S0-ADG-718

A Note to Parents and Teachers

DK READERS is a compelling program for beginning readers, designed in conjunction with leading literacy experts, including Dr. Linda Gambrell, Professor of Education at Clemson University. Dr. Gambrell has served as President of the National Reading Conference and the College Reading Association, and has recently been elected to serve as President of the International Reading Association.

Beautiful illustrations and superb full-color photographs combine with engaging, easy-to-read stories to offer a fresh approach to each subject in the series.

Each DK READER is guaranteed to capture a child's interest while developing his or her reading skills, general knowledge, and love of reading.

The five levels of DK READERS are aimed at different reading abilities, enabling you to choose the books that are exactly right for your child:

Pre-level 1: Learning to read
Level 1: Beginning to read
Level 2: Beginning to read alone
Level 3: Reading alone
Level 4: Proficient readers

The "normal" age at which a child begins to read can be anywhere from three to eight years old. Adult participation through the lower levels is very helpful for providing encouragement, discussing storylines, and sounding out unfamiliar words.

No matter which level you select, you can be sure that you are helping your child learn to read, then read to learn!

LONDON, NEW YORK, MUNICH,
MELBOURNE, AND DELHI

Editor Kate Simkins
Designers Cathy Tincknell
and John Kelly
Senior Editor Catherine Saunders
Brand Manager Lisa Lanzarini
Publishing Manager Simon Beecroft
Category Publisher Alex Allan
DTP Designer Hanna Ländin
Production Rochelle Talary
Reading Consultant Linda Gambrell

First American Edition, 2007
Published in the United States by
DK Publishing
375 Hudson Street
New York, New York 10014

07 08 09 10 10 9 8 7 6 5 4 3 2 1

Copyright © 2007 Dorling Kindersley Limited

Some material contained in this book was previously published in
2003 in *Tales of the Dead: Ancient Egypt.*

Published in Great Britain by Dorling Kindersley Limited.

DK books are available at special discounts for bulk purchases for
sales promotion, premiums, fund-raising, or educational use.
For details contact: DK Publishing Special Markets,
375 Hudson Street, New York, NY 10014

A Cataloging-in-Publication record for this book is available from
the Library of Congress.

ISBN 978-0-7566-2563-4 (paperback)
ISBN 978-0-7566-2564-1 (hardcover)

All artwork by Inklink except the illustrations of the town, the
temple, and the pharaoh on page 42, the servant, marriage contract,
prisoners, Chief Embalmer, and Lord Ini's Palace on page 43, the
pyramid, burial chamber, and the robbers on page 44, the soldiers
and the House of the Dead on page 45, the priest and the temple on
page 46, and the natron table on page 48 by Richard Bonson.

Discover more at
www.dk.com

Contents

DK READERS

PROFICIENT
4
READERS

CURSE of the CROCODILE GOD

Written by Stewart Ross
Illustrated by Inklink

DK Publishing

Curse Of The Crocodile God

Methen's story takes place 4,000 years ago in Ancient Egypt. It is the year 1795 BCE, and the ruler of Egypt is Pharaoh Sobekneferu. Our hero and his new friend Madja live in a town near Hawara in northern Egypt. Turn to page 42 to see a map of Ancient Egypt and a timeline, then let the story begin....

"My name is Methen, and this is my friend Madja. Our lives are in great danger! We are caught in a fiendish plot hatched by a corrupt official. As the son of a respected priest, nothing in my life has prepared me for this. My days have been spent at scribe school, learning to read and write. Madja is a servant girl in a nobleman's court. Like me, she is 13 years old, but our paths had never crossed until the evening of the banquet at Lord Ini's palace."

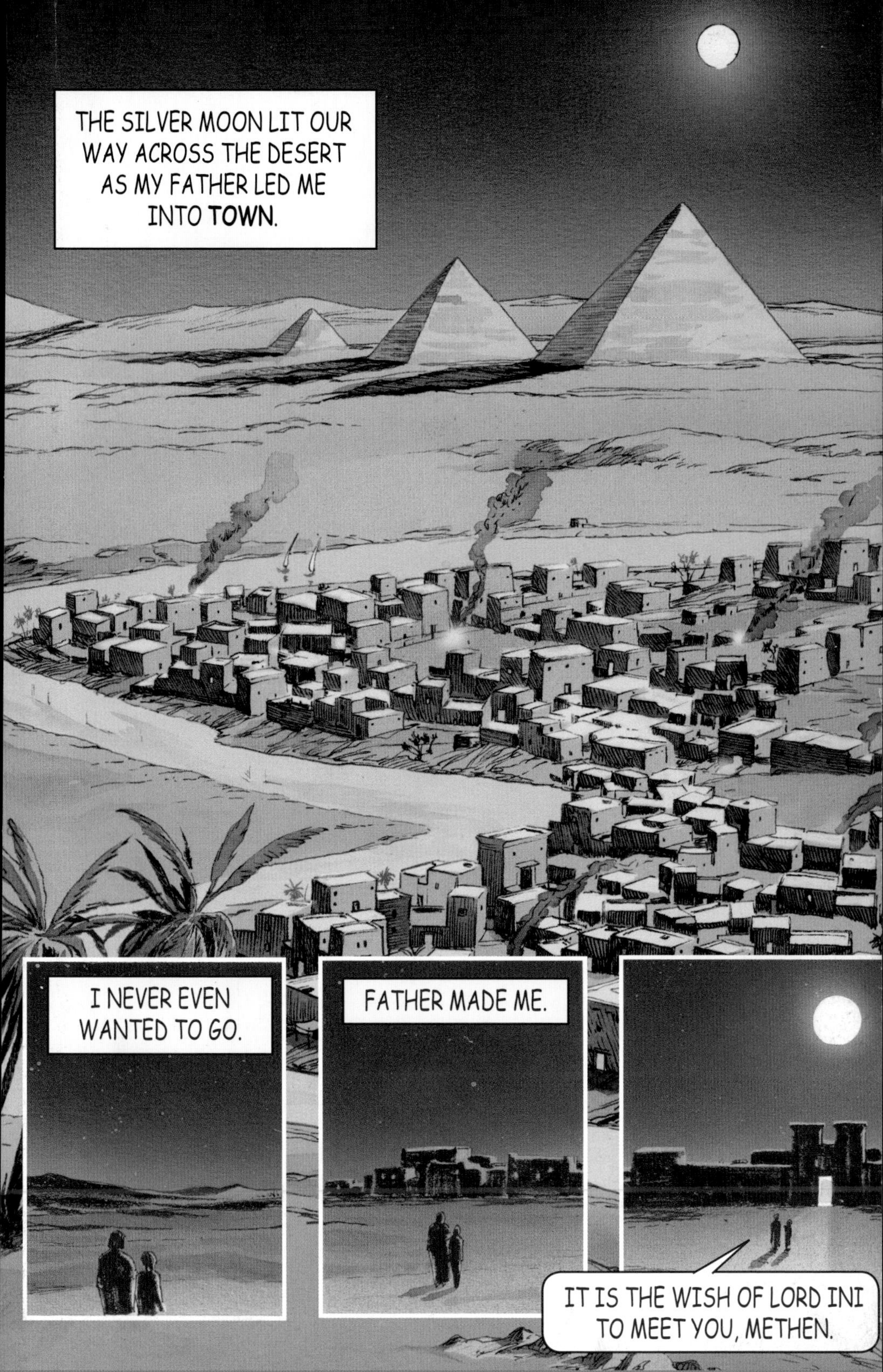
THE SILVER MOON LIT OUR WAY ACROSS THE DESERT AS MY FATHER LED ME INTO **TOWN**.
I NEVER EVEN WANTED TO GO.
FATHER MADE ME.
IT IS THE WISH OF LORD INI TO MEET YOU, METHEN.

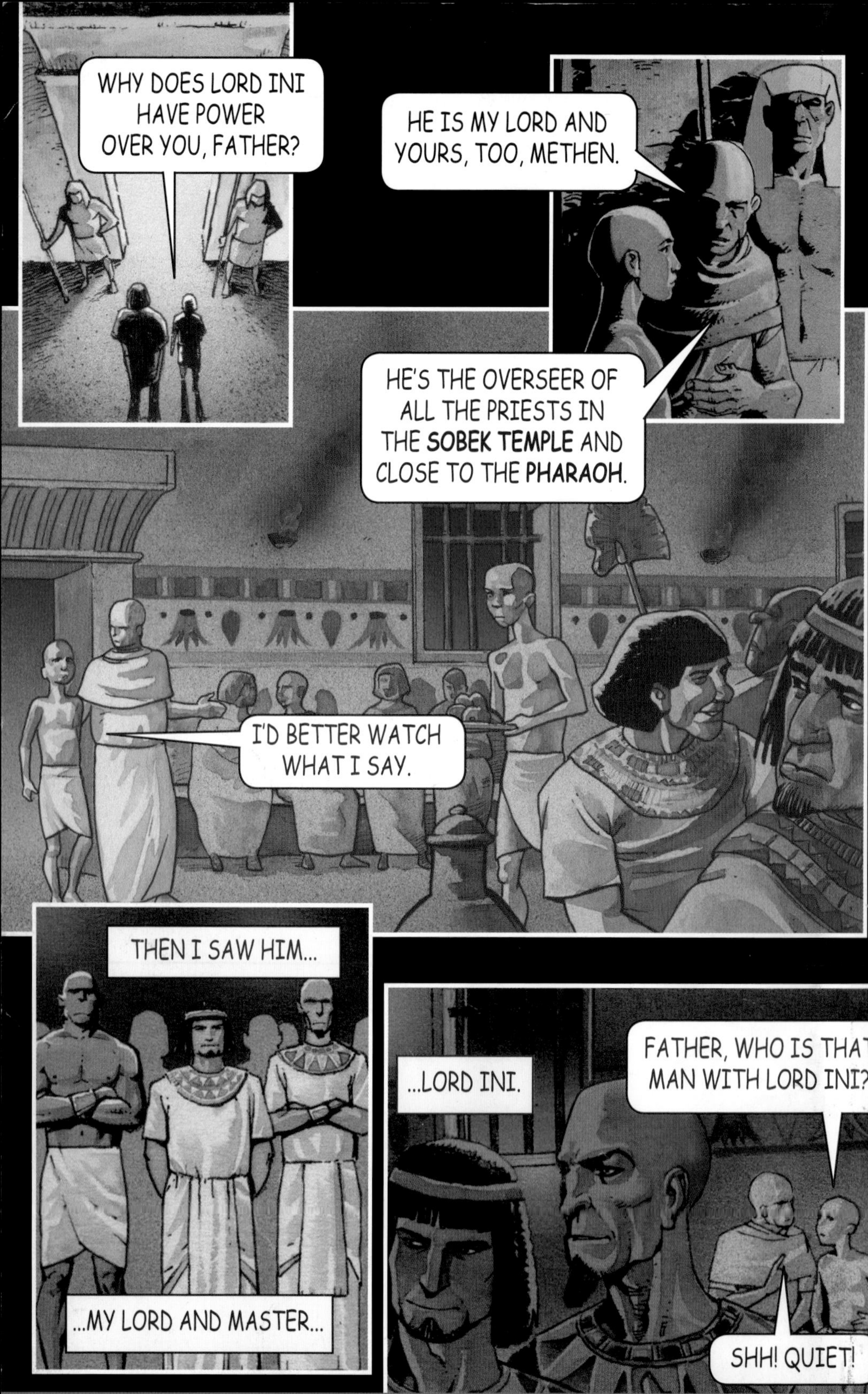
WHY DOES LORD INI HAVE POWER OVER YOU, FATHER?
HE IS MY LORD AND YOURS, TOO, METHEN.
HE'S THE OVERSEER OF ALL THE PRIESTS IN THE **SOBEK TEMPLE** AND CLOSE TO THE **PHARAOH**.
I'D BETTER WATCH WHAT I SAY.
THEN I SAW HIM...
...MY LORD AND MASTER...
...LORD INI.
FATHER, WHO IS THAT MAN WITH LORD INI?
SHH! QUIET!

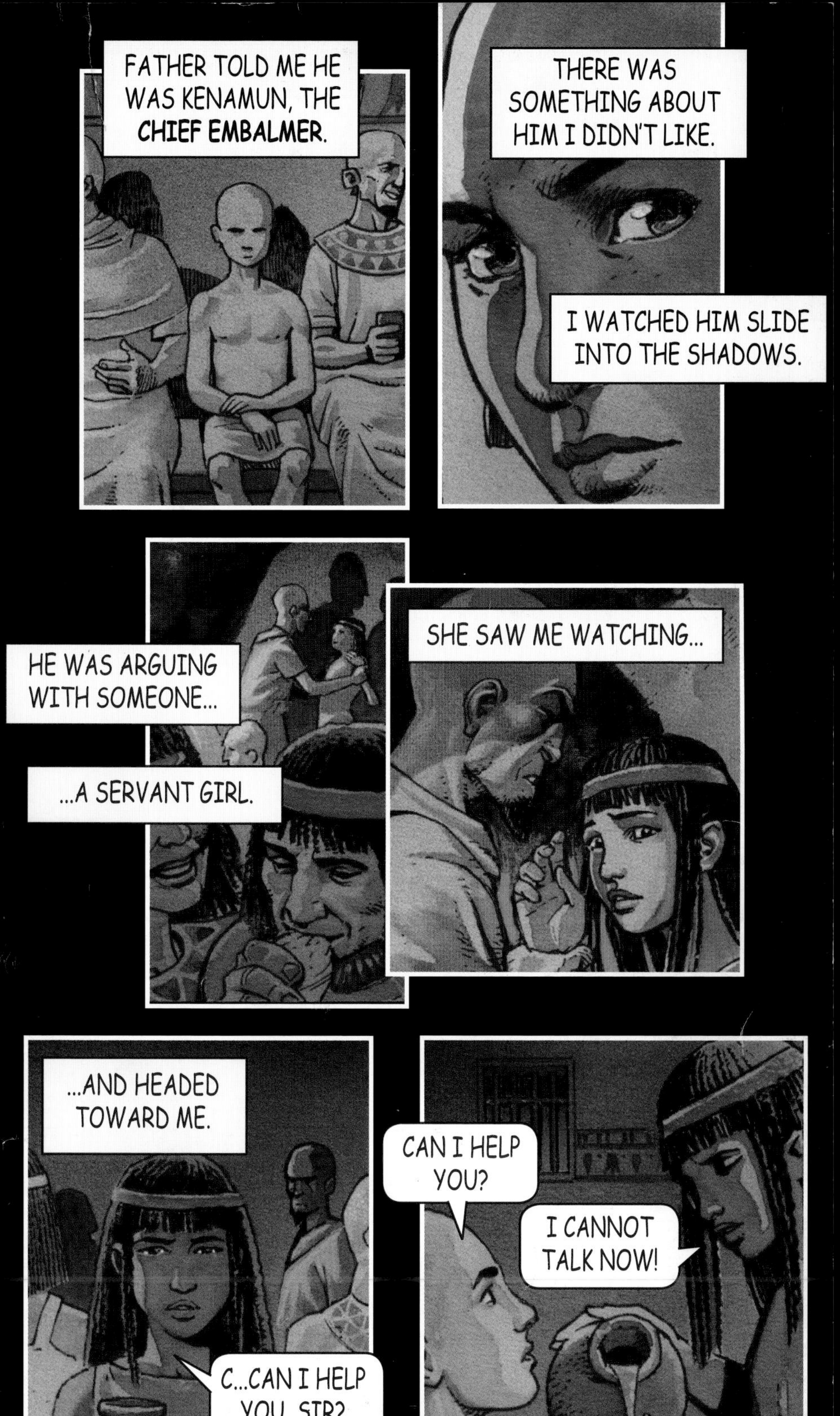
FATHER TOLD ME HE WAS KENAMUN, THE **CHIEF EMBALMER**.
THERE WAS SOMETHING ABOUT HIM I DIDN'T LIKE.
I WATCHED HIM SLIDE INTO THE SHADOWS.
HE WAS ARGUING WITH SOMEONE...
...A SERVANT GIRL.
SHE SAW ME WATCHING...
...AND HEADED TOWARD ME.
C...CAN I HELP YOU, SIR?
CAN I HELP YOU?
I CANNOT TALK NOW!

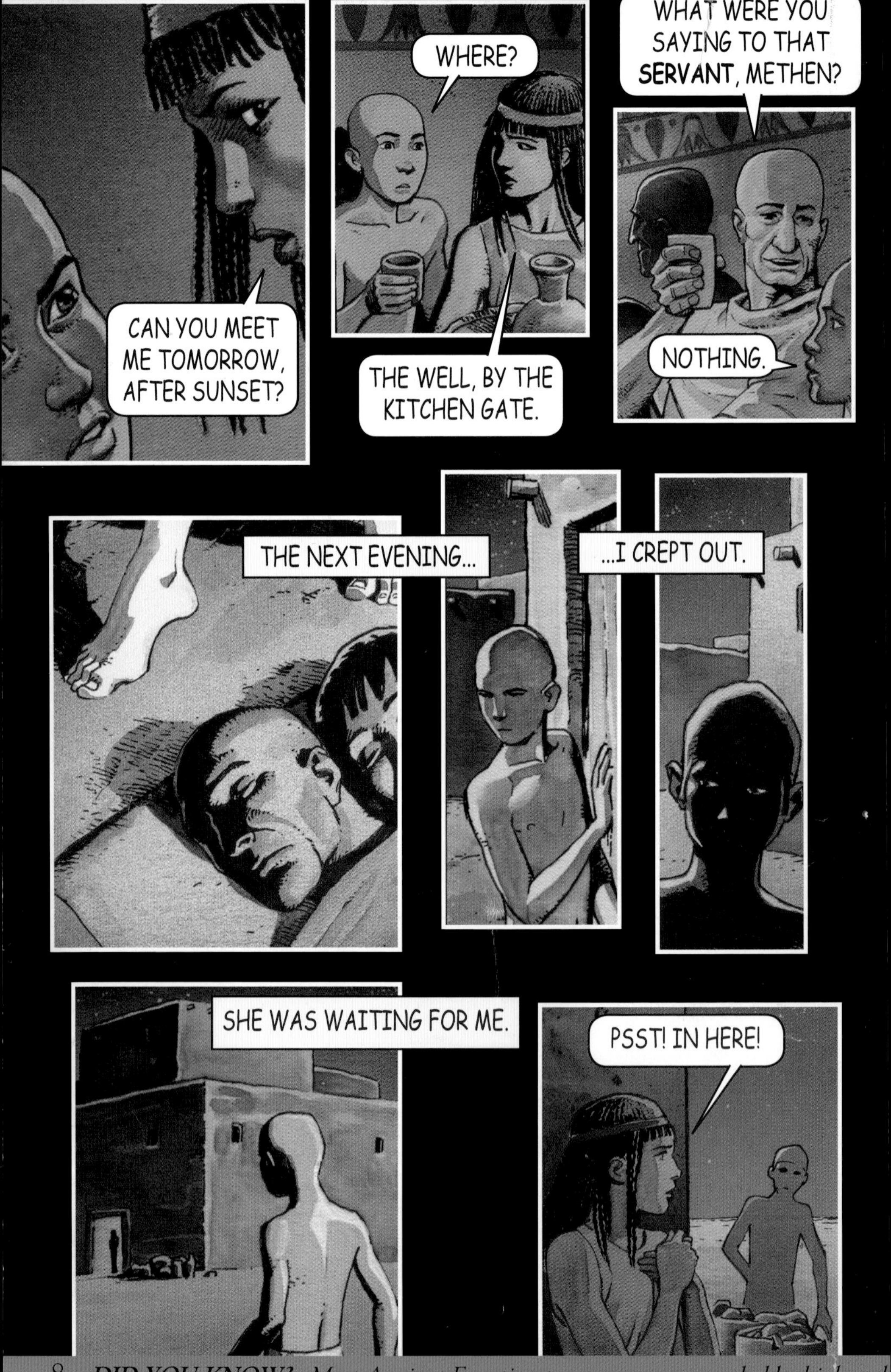
CAN YOU MEET ME TOMORROW, AFTER SUNSET?
WHERE?
THE WELL, BY THE KITCHEN GATE.
WHAT WERE YOU SAYING TO THAT **SERVANT**, METHEN?
NOTHING.
THE NEXT EVENING...
...I CREPT OUT.
SHE WAS WAITING FOR ME.
PSST! IN HERE!

 DID YOU KNOW? *Most Ancient Egyptian towns were surrounded by high wall*

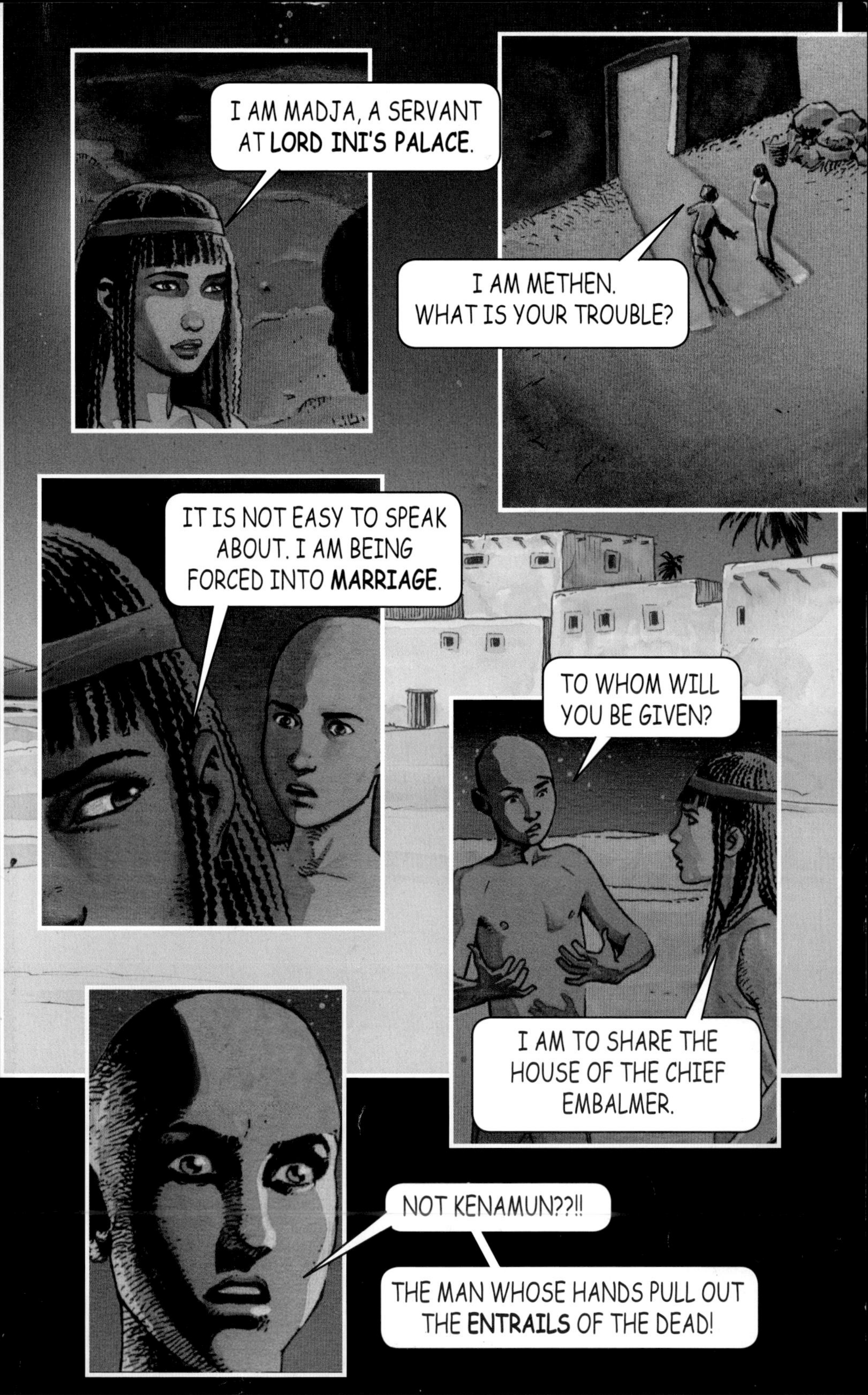
I AM MADJA, A SERVANT AT LORD INI'S PALACE.
I AM METHEN. WHAT IS YOUR TROUBLE?
IT IS NOT EASY TO SPEAK ABOUT. I AM BEING FORCED INTO MARRIAGE.
TO WHOM WILL YOU BE GIVEN?
I AM TO SHARE THE HOUSE OF THE CHIEF EMBALMER.
NOT KENAMUN??!!
THE MAN WHOSE HANDS PULL OUT THE ENTRAILS OF THE DEAD!

The houses had flat roofs, which were used as an extra room.

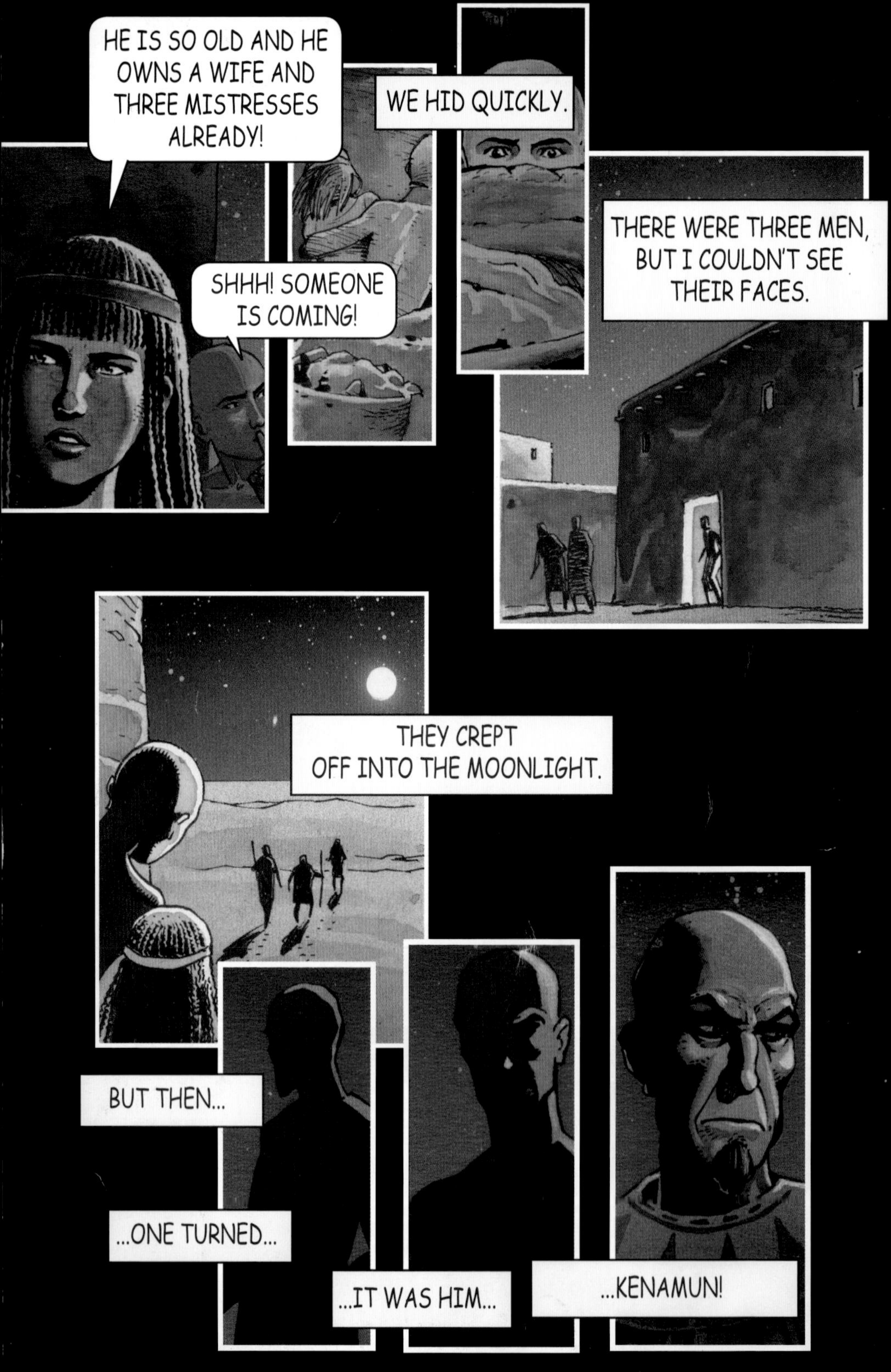
HE IS SO OLD AND HE OWNS A WIFE AND THREE MISTRESSES ALREADY!
SHHH! SOMEONE IS COMING!
WE HID QUICKLY.
THERE WERE THREE MEN, BUT I COULDN'T SEE THEIR FACES.
THEY CREPT OFF INTO THE MOONLIGHT.
BUT THEN...
...ONE TURNED...
...IT WAS HIM...
...KENAMUN!

DID YOU KNOW? *The first Egyptian pyramid was built in 2650 BCE.*

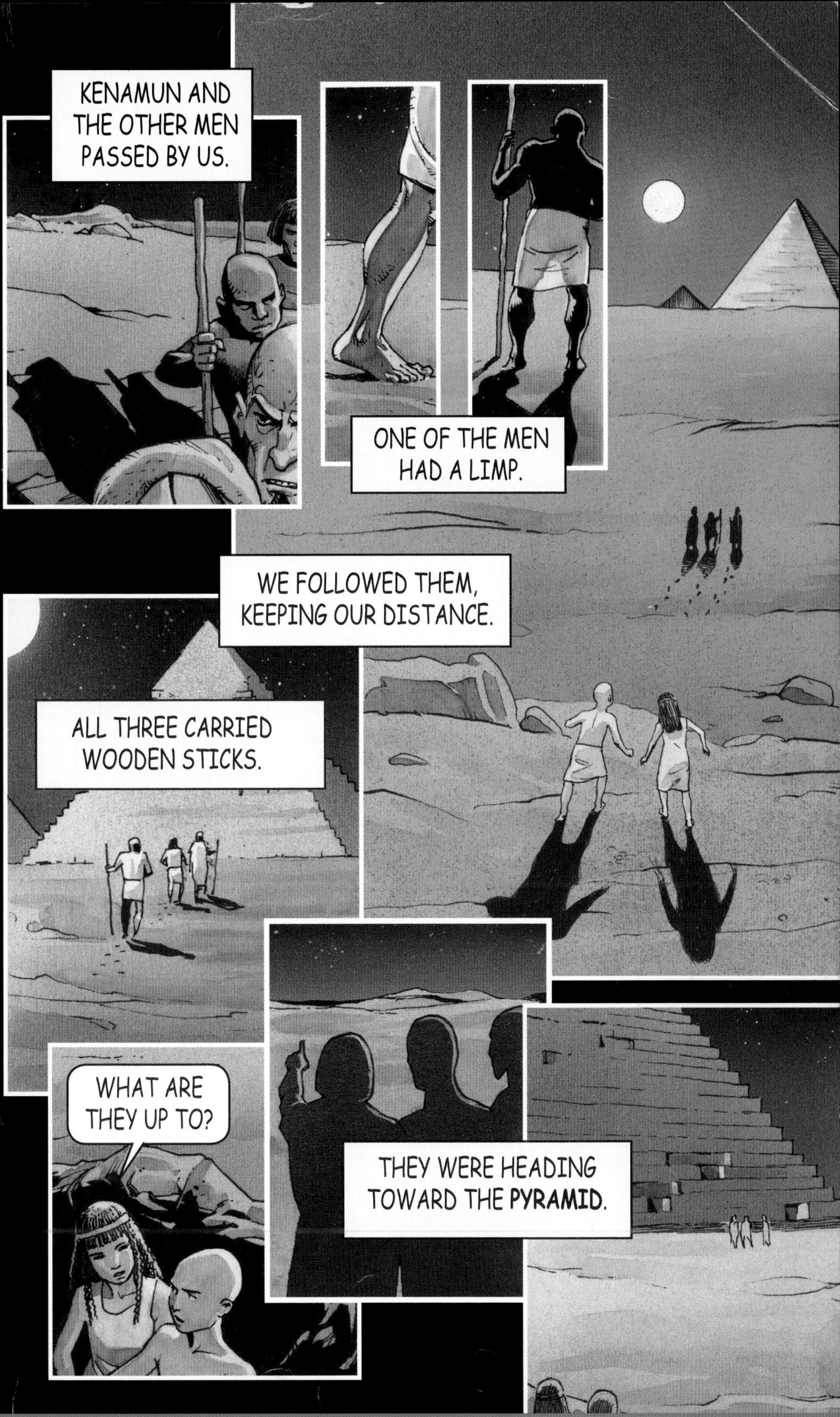
KENAMUN AND THE OTHER MEN PASSED BY US.
ONE OF THE MEN HAD A LIMP.
WE FOLLOWED THEM, KEEPING OUR DISTANCE.
ALL THREE CARRIED WOODEN STICKS.
WHAT ARE THEY UP TO?
THEY WERE HEADING TOWARD THE **PYRAMID**.

Pyramids have a square base and four triangular sides.

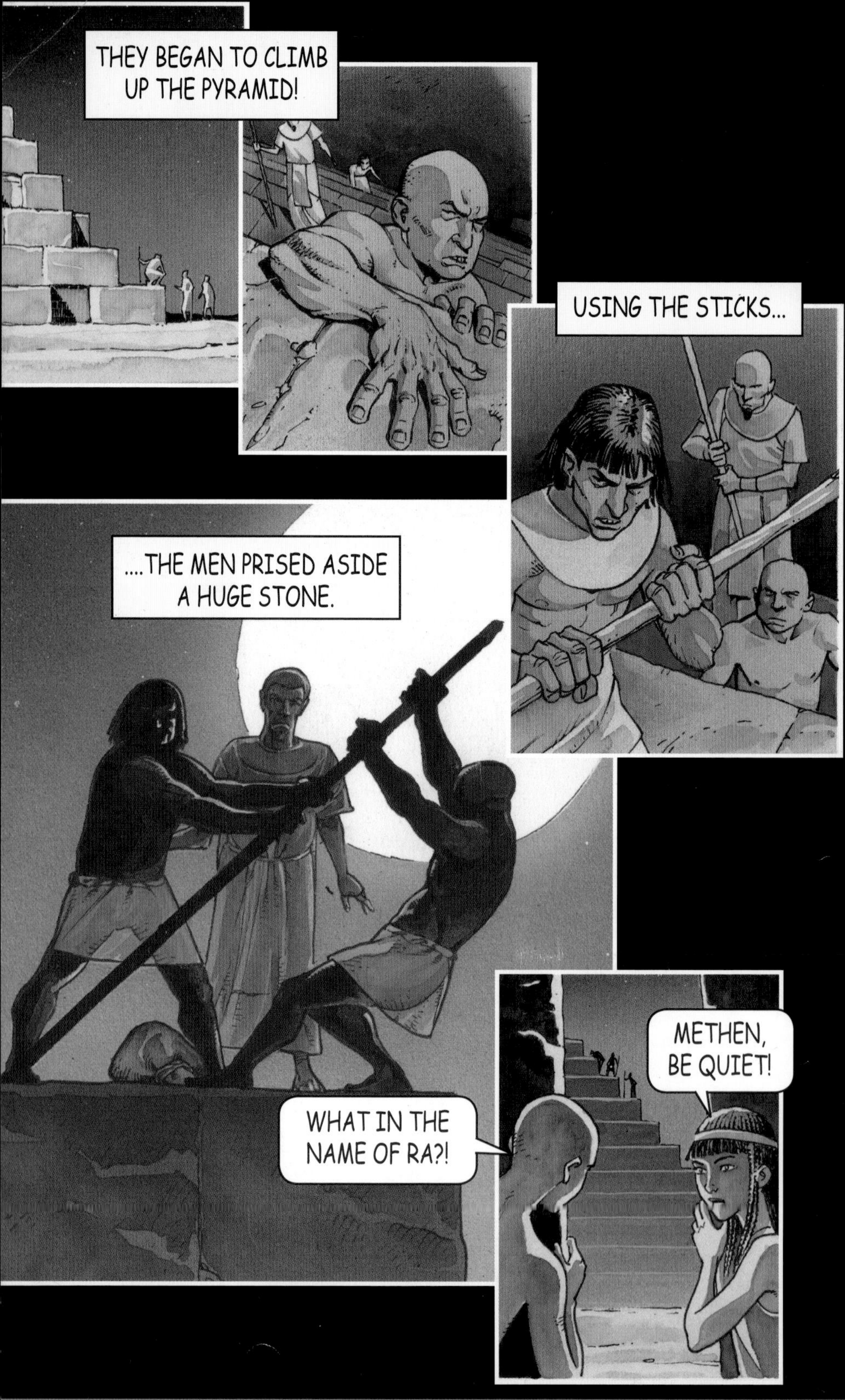
THEY BEGAN TO CLIMB UP THE PYRAMID!
USING THE STICKS...
....THE MEN PRISED ASIDE A HUGE STONE.
WHAT IN THE NAME OF RA?!
METHEN, BE QUIET!

DID YOU KNOW? *Ra was the Sun god.*

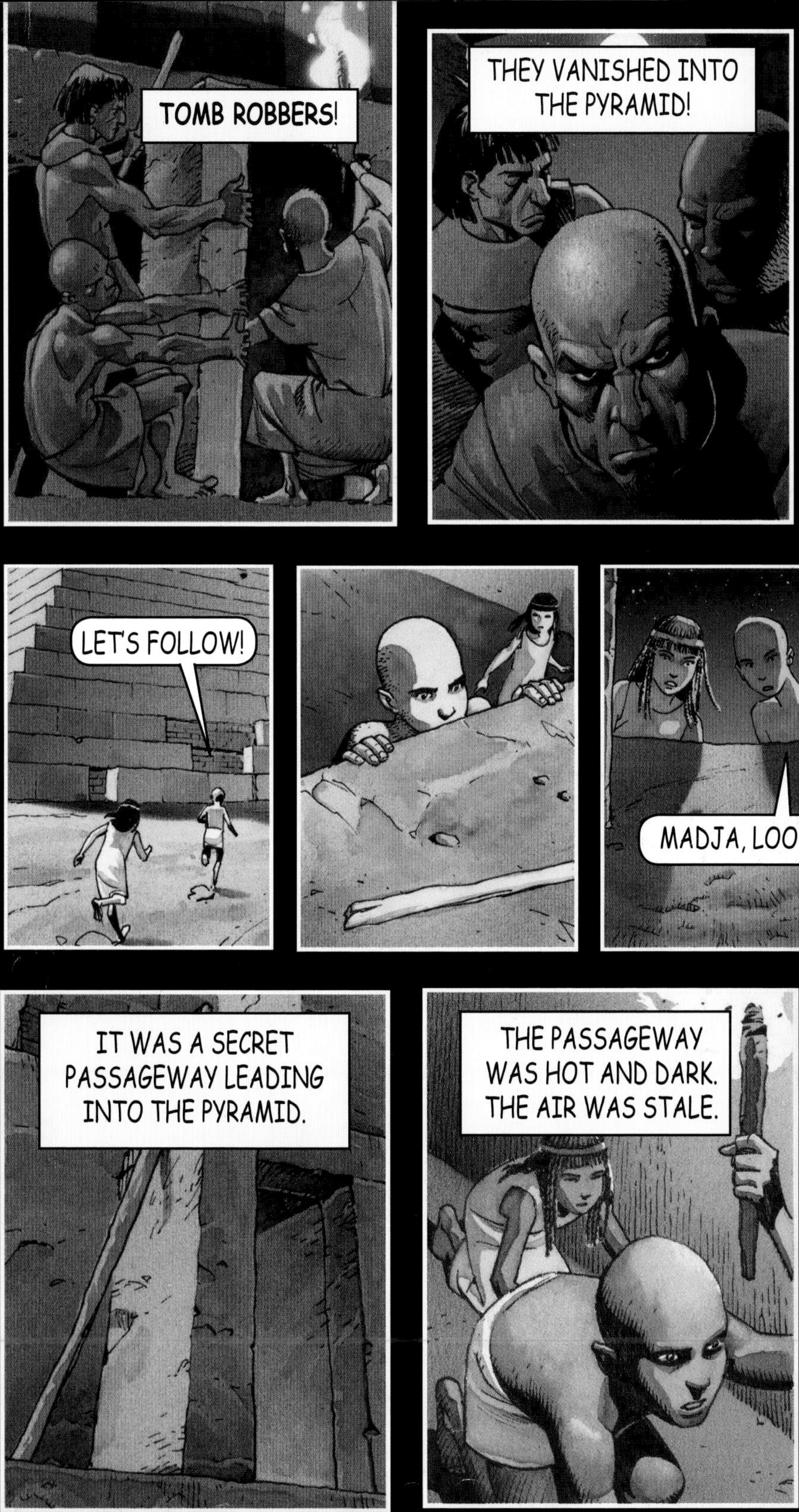
TOMB ROBBERS!
THEY VANISHED INTO THE PYRAMID!
LET'S FOLLOW!
MADJA, LOOK!
IT WAS A SECRET PASSAGEWAY LEADING INTO THE PYRAMID.
THE PASSAGEWAY WAS HOT AND DARK. THE AIR WAS STALE.

The Great Pyramid was made of more than 2 million stone blocks.

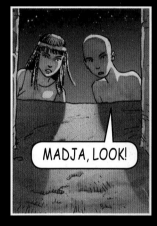

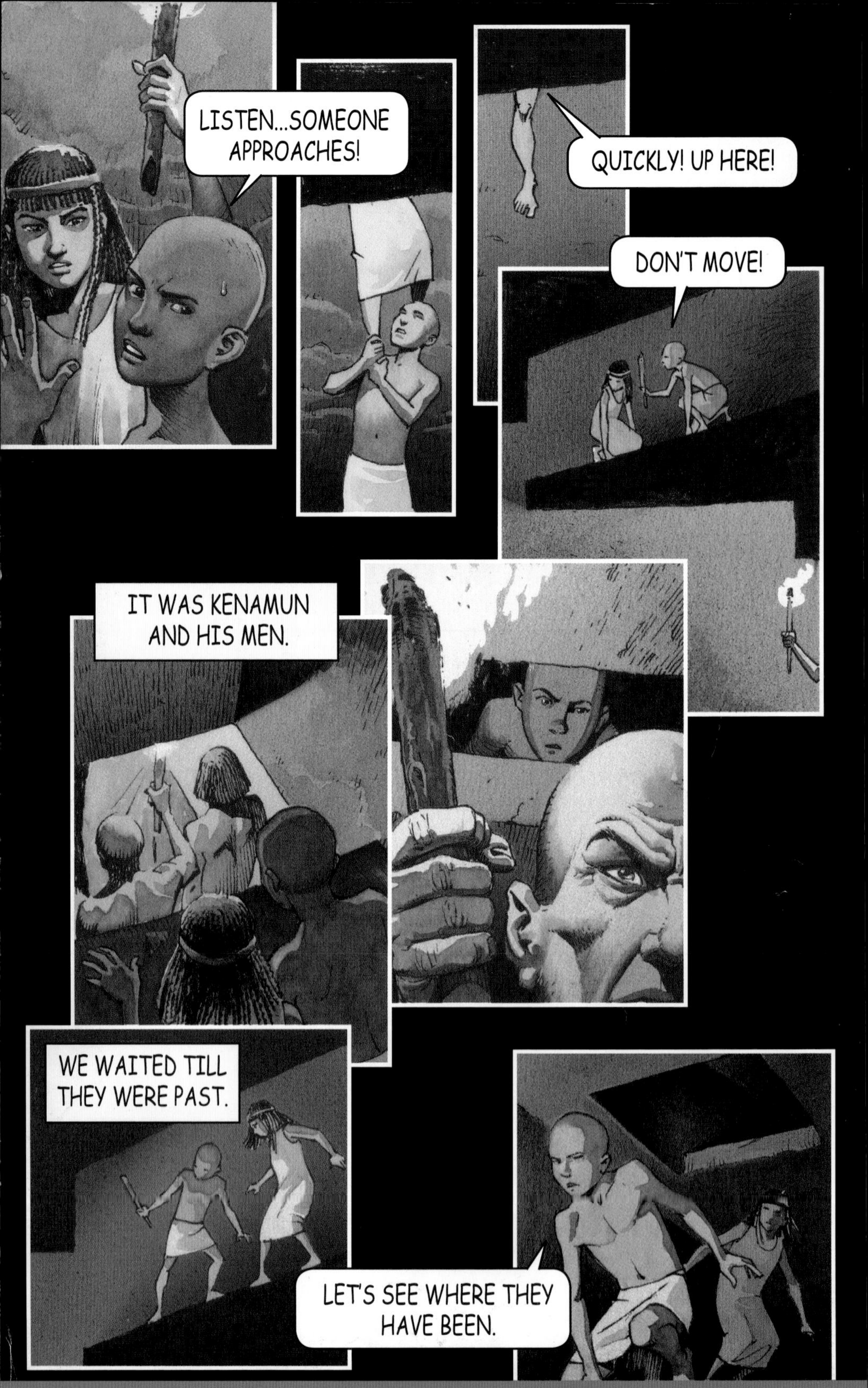
LISTEN...SOMEONE APPROACHES!
QUICKLY! UP HERE!
DON'T MOVE!
IT WAS KENAMUN AND HIS MEN.
WE WAITED TILL THEY WERE PAST.
LET'S SEE WHERE THEY HAVE BEEN.

 DID YOU KNOW? *Pyramids had trap doors to capture robbers.*

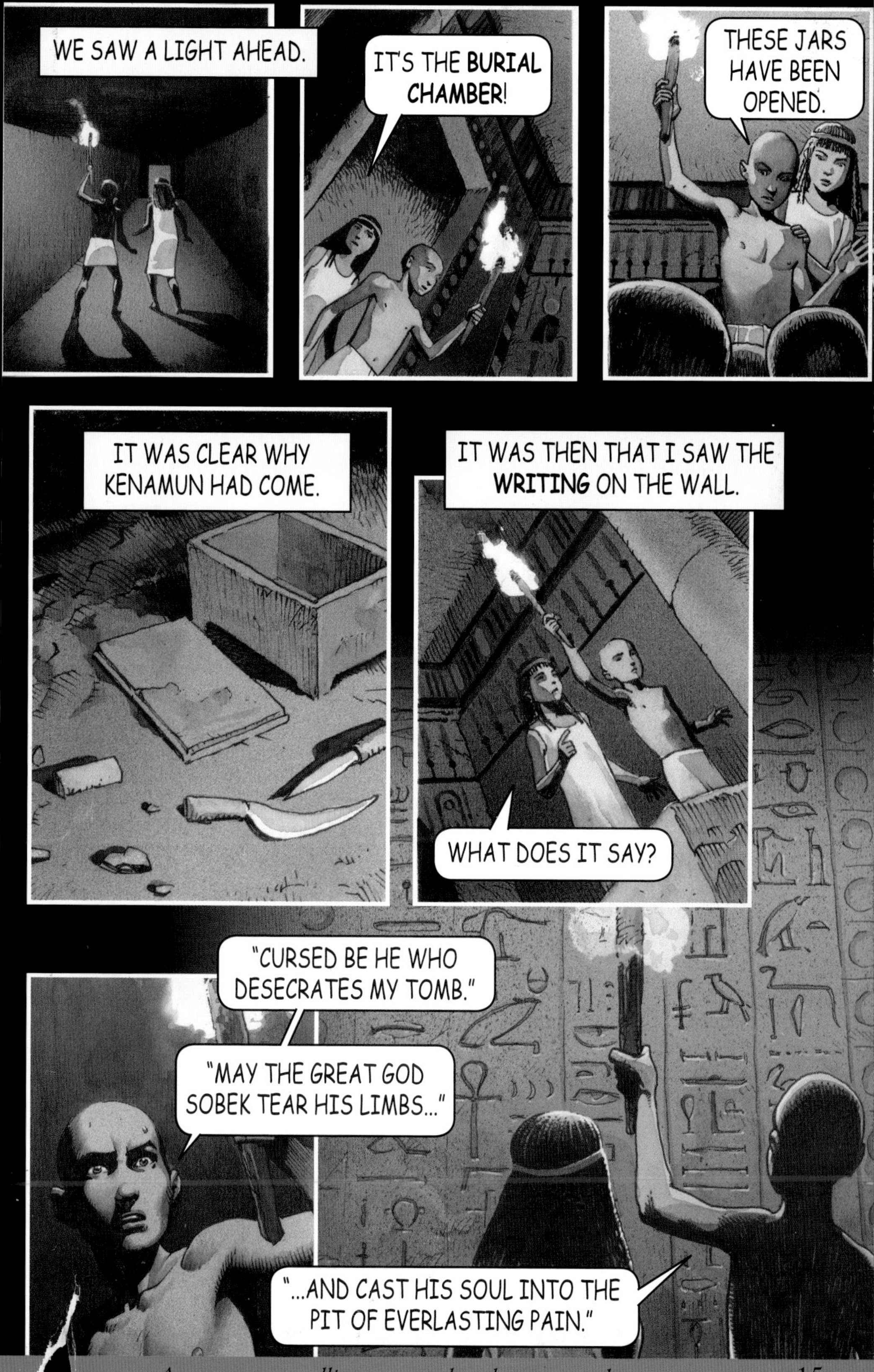
WE SAW A LIGHT AHEAD.
IT'S THE BURIAL CHAMBER!
THESE JARS HAVE BEEN OPENED.
IT WAS CLEAR WHY KENAMUN HAD COME.
IT WAS THEN THAT I SAW THE WRITING ON THE WALL.
WHAT DOES IT SAY?
"CURSED BE HE WHO DESECRATES MY TOMB."
"MAY THE GREAT GOD SOBEK TEAR HIS LIMBS..."
"...AND CAST HIS SOUL INTO THE PIT OF EVERLASTING PAIN."

A curse was a calling on a god to do someone harm.

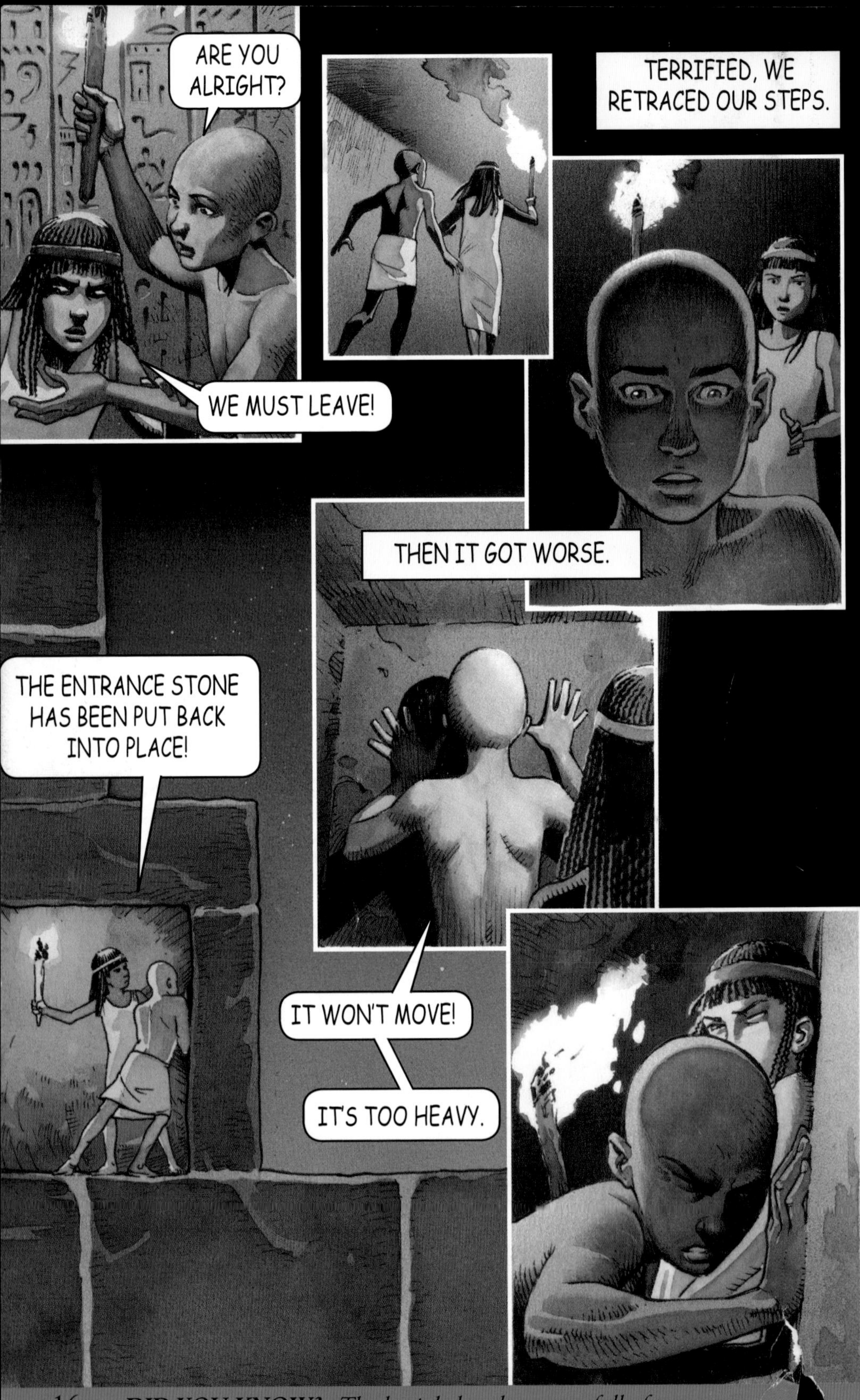
ARE YOU ALRIGHT?
WE MUST LEAVE!
TERRIFIED, WE RETRACED OUR STEPS.
THEN IT GOT WORSE.
THE ENTRANCE STONE HAS BEEN PUT BACK INTO PLACE!
IT WON'T MOVE!
IT'S TOO HEAVY.

 DID YOU KNOW? *The burial chambers were full of treasure.*

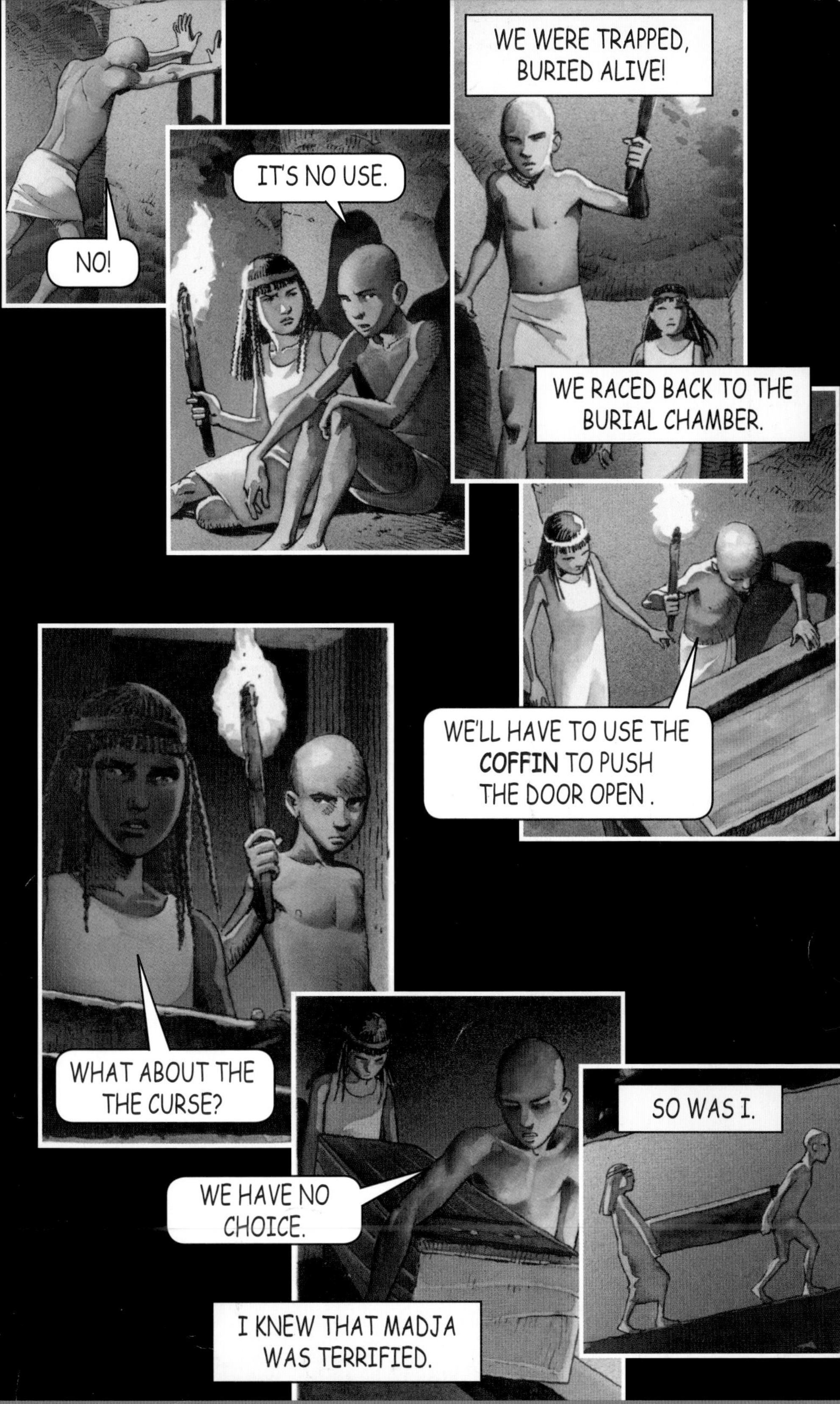
NO!
IT'S NO USE.
WE WERE TRAPPED, BURIED ALIVE!
WE RACED BACK TO THE BURIAL CHAMBER.
WE'LL HAVE TO USE THE **COFFIN** TO PUSH THE DOOR OPEN .
WHAT ABOUT THE THE CURSE?
WE HAVE NO CHOICE.
I KNEW THAT MADJA WAS TERRIFIED.
SO WAS I.

The massive stone blocks weighed about 2 tons (2 metric tons).

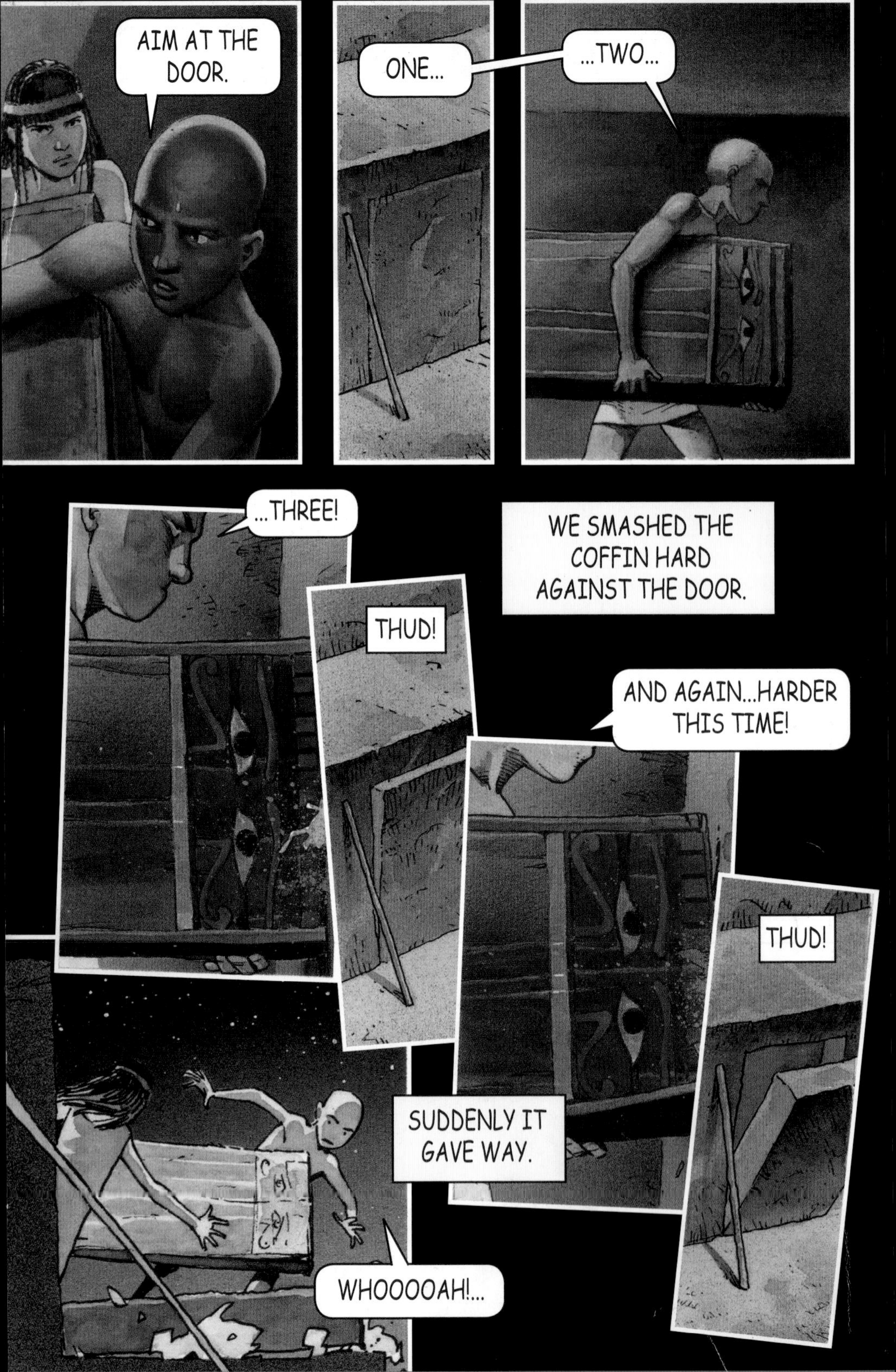
AIM AT THE DOOR.
ONE...
...TWO...
...THREE!
WE SMASHED THE COFFIN HARD AGAINST THE DOOR.
THUD!
AND AGAIN...HARDER THIS TIME!
THUD!
SUDDENLY IT GAVE WAY.
WHOOOOAH!...

 DID YOU KNOW? *In Ancient Egypt, eyes were a symbol of protection.*

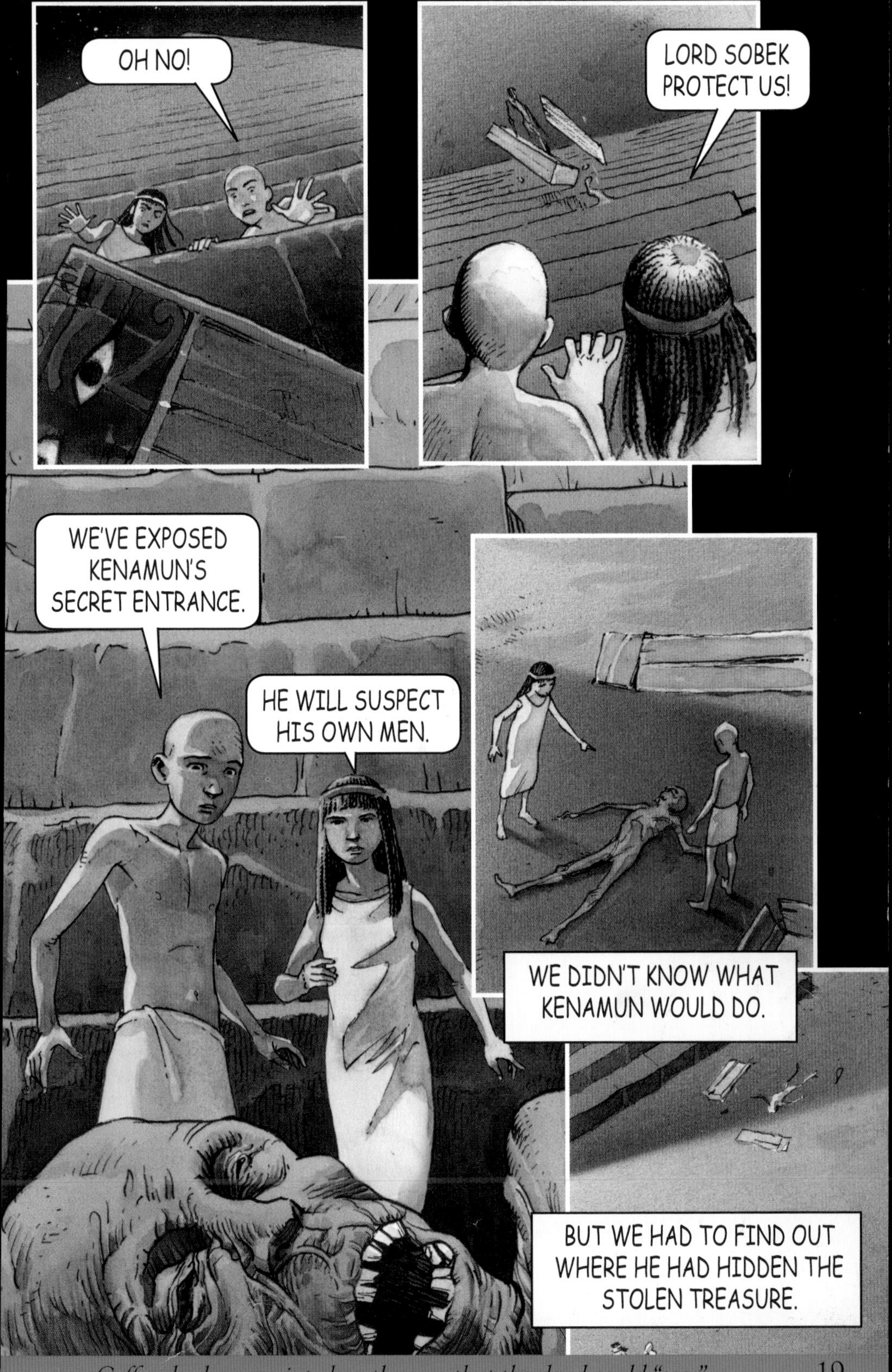
OH NO!
LORD SOBEK PROTECT US!
WE'VE EXPOSED KENAMUN'S SECRET ENTRANCE.
HE WILL SUSPECT HIS OWN MEN.
WE DIDN'T KNOW WHAT KENAMUN WOULD DO.
BUT WE HAD TO FIND OUT WHERE HE HAD HIDDEN THE STOLEN TREASURE.

Coffins had eyes painted on them so that the dead could "see."

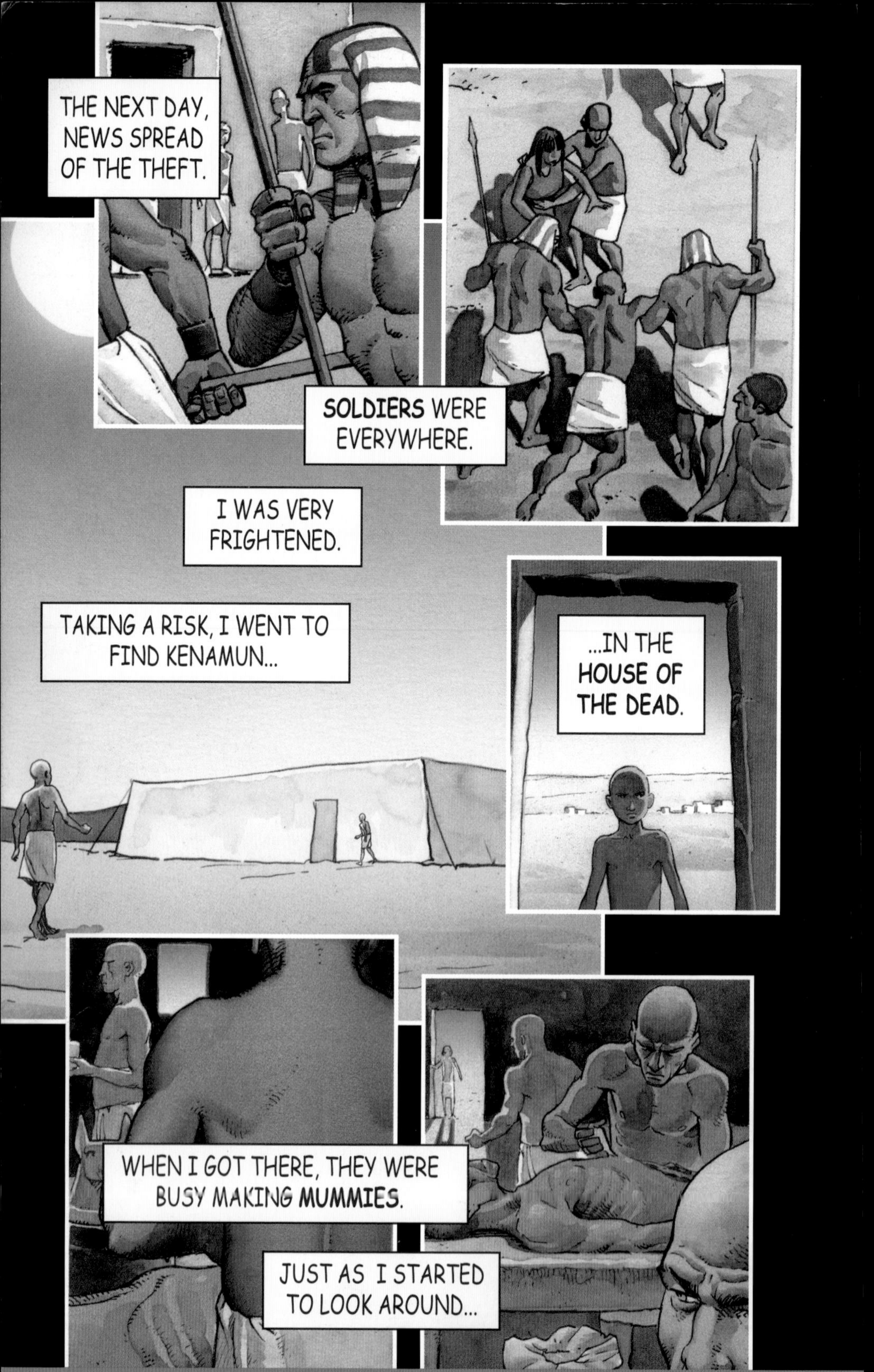
THE NEXT DAY, NEWS SPREAD OF THE THEFT.
SOLDIERS WERE EVERYWHERE.
I WAS VERY FRIGHTENED.
TAKING A RISK, I WENT TO FIND KENAMUN...
...IN THE HOUSE OF THE DEAD.
WHEN I GOT THERE, THEY WERE BUSY MAKING MUMMIES.
JUST AS I STARTED TO LOOK AROUND...

DID YOU KNOW? *It took 70 days to make a mummy.*

...THE FOREMAN GRABBED ME.

YOU'D BETTER LEAVE, BOY!

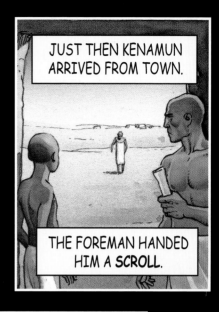

JUST THEN KENAMUN ARRIVED FROM TOWN.

THE FOREMAN HANDED HIM A **SCROLL**.

IT MUST HAVE BEEN ABOUT THE MESS AT THE PYRAMID.

KENAMUN MUST THINK THAT HIS OWN MEN...

...HAD GONE BACK FOR THEIR OWN GAIN!

I'LL TEACH THEM TO CROSS ME!

WHAT ARE YOU DOING HERE, BOY?

GET OUT!

Anubis was the god of embalming (making mummies).

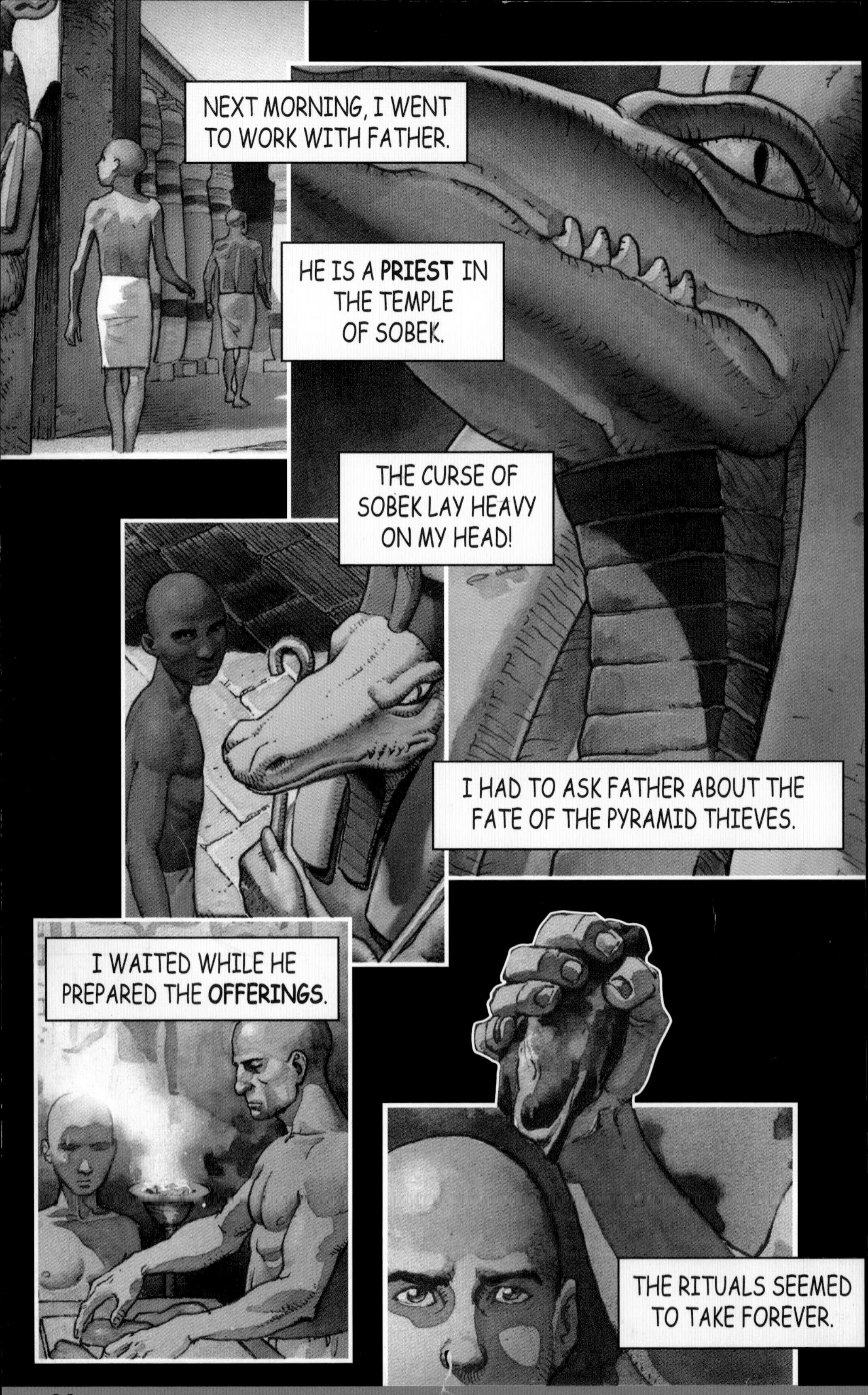
NEXT MORNING, I WENT TO WORK WITH FATHER.
HE IS A **PRIEST** IN THE TEMPLE OF SOBEK.
THE CURSE OF SOBEK LAY HEAVY ON MY HEAD!
I HAD TO ASK FATHER ABOUT THE FATE OF THE PYRAMID THIEVES.
I WAITED WHILE HE PREPARED THE **OFFERINGS**.
THE RITUALS SEEMED TO TAKE FOREVER.

 DID YOU KNOW? *Sobek was half man, half crocodile.*

I COULDN'T WAIT ANY LONGER.
I ASKED FATHER.
HE ANSWERED, "SOBEK WILL BE **AVENGED**!"
BUT MADJA AND I HAD COMMITTED **SACRILEGE**, TOO.
WE HOPED SOBEK WOULD HAVE MERCY ON US!

Real crocodiles lived in the Temple of Sobek.

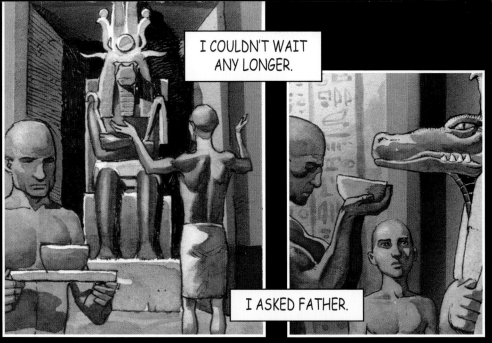

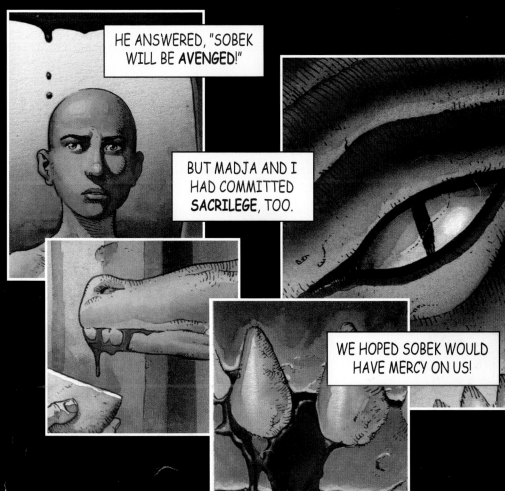

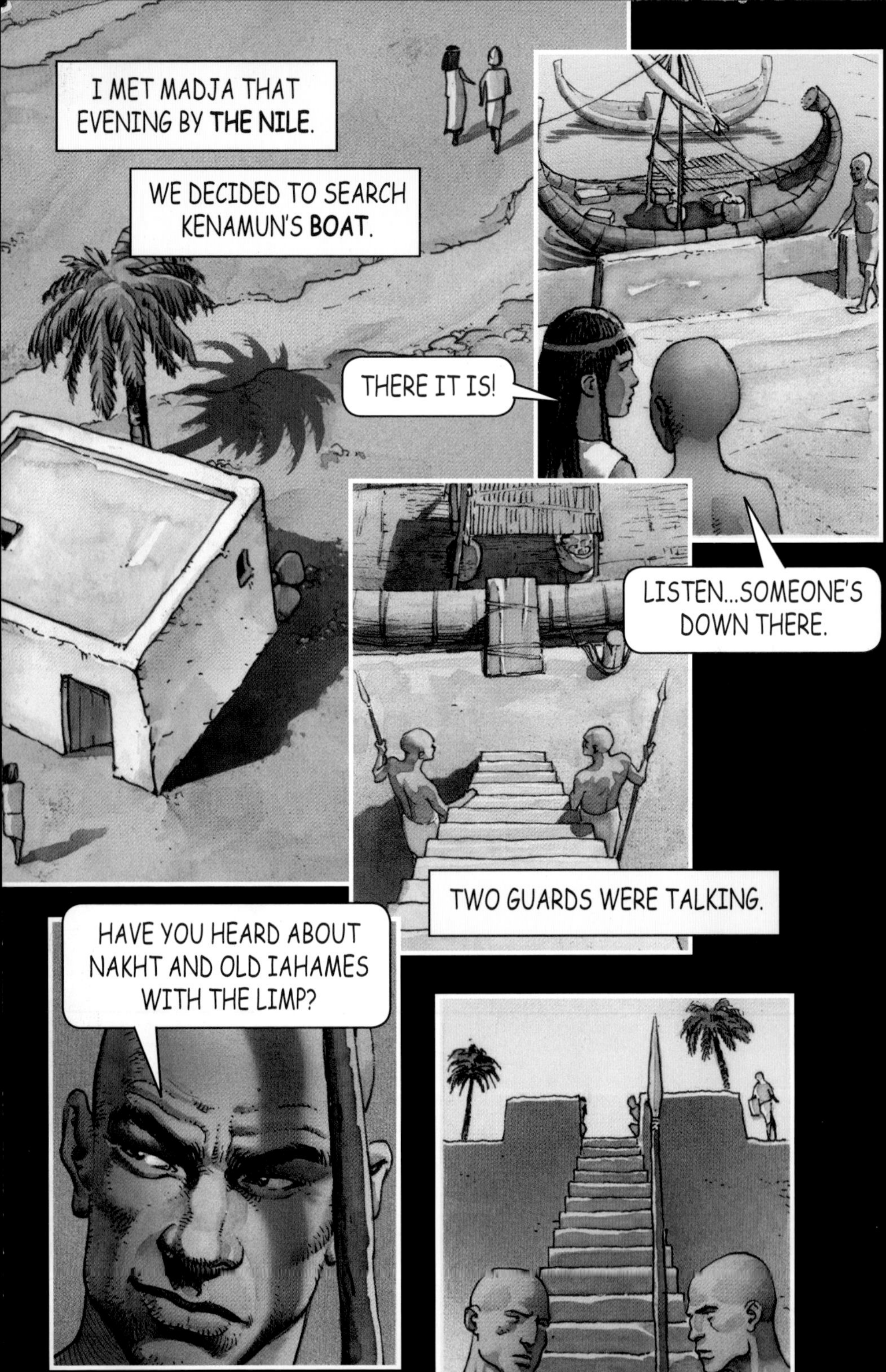
I MET MADJA THAT EVENING BY THE NILE.
WE DECIDED TO SEARCH KENAMUN'S BOAT.
THERE IT IS!
LISTEN...SOMEONE'S DOWN THERE.
TWO GUARDS WERE TALKING.
HAVE YOU HEARD ABOUT NAKHT AND OLD IAHAMES WITH THE LIMP?
NO, WHAT'S HAPPENED?

 DID YOU KNOW? *Ancient Egypt grew up alongside the Nile River.*

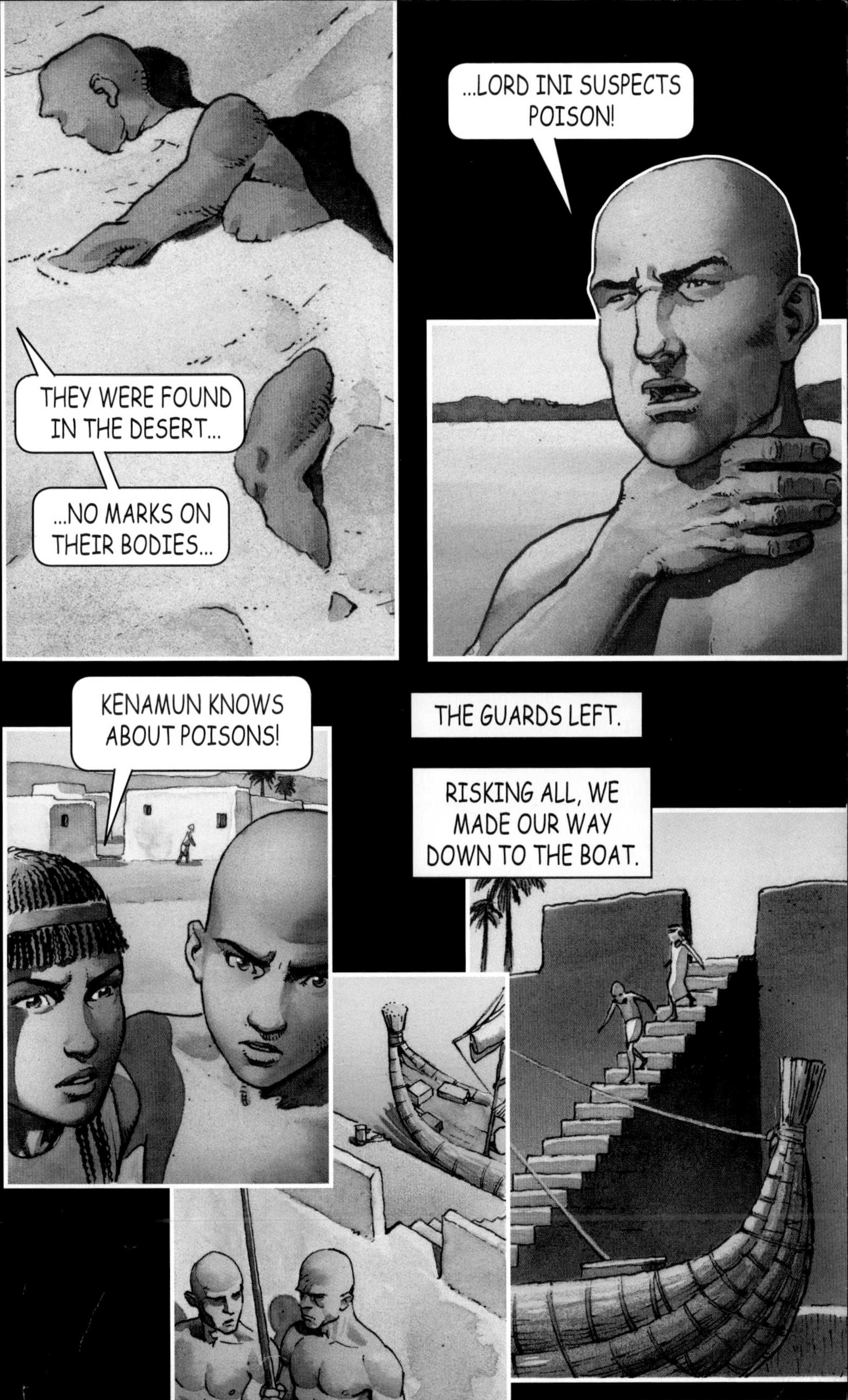
THEY WERE FOUND IN THE DESERT...
...NO MARKS ON THEIR BODIES...
...LORD INI SUSPECTS POISON!
KENAMUN KNOWS ABOUT POISONS!
THE GUARDS LEFT.
RISKING ALL, WE MADE OUR WAY DOWN TO THE BOAT.

People in Ancient Egypt went almost everywhere by boat.

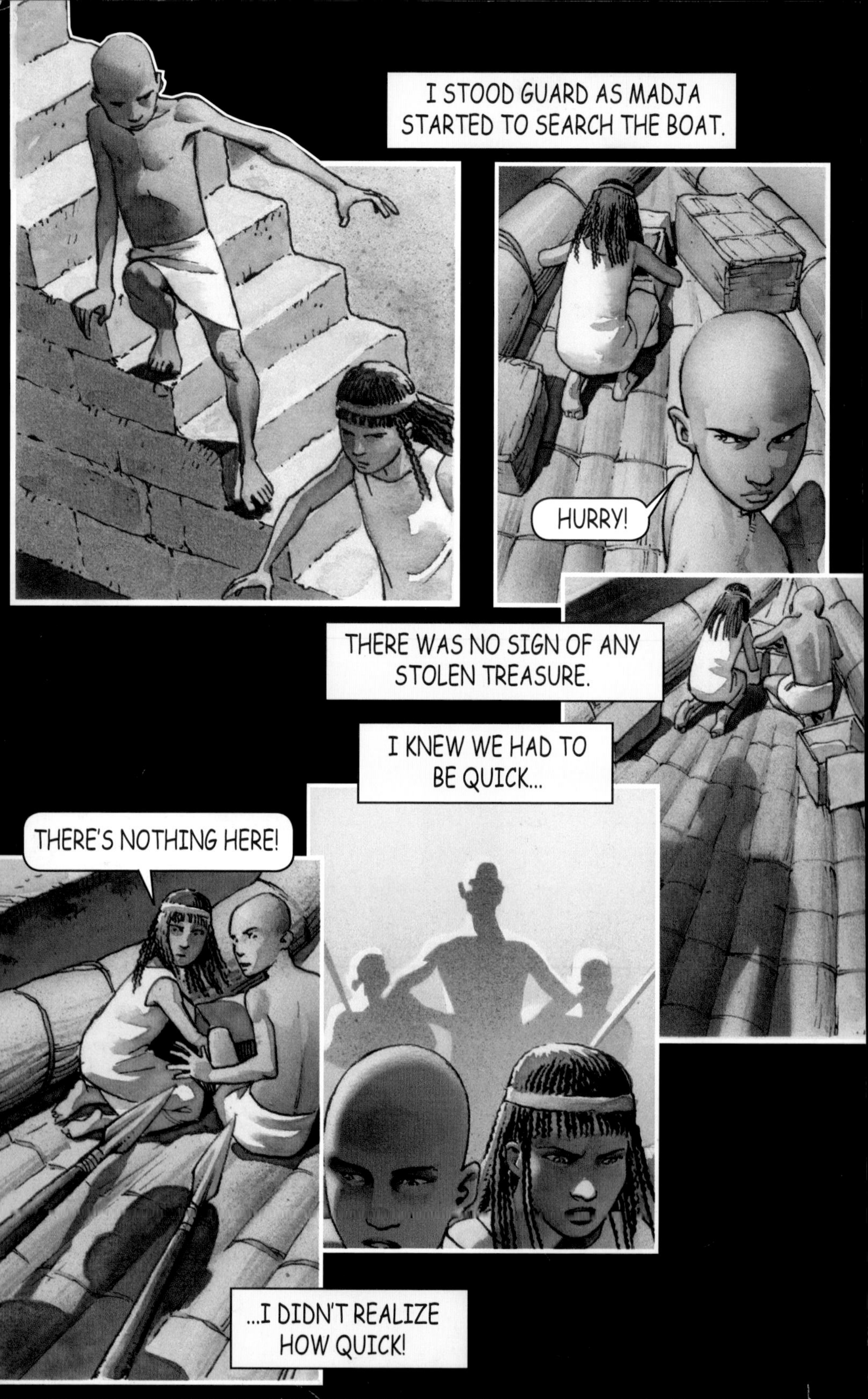
I STOOD GUARD AS MADJA STARTED TO SEARCH THE BOAT.
HURRY!
THERE WAS NO SIGN OF ANY STOLEN TREASURE.
I KNEW WE HAD TO BE QUICK...
THERE'S NOTHING HERE!
...I DIDN'T REALIZE HOW QUICK!

 DID YOU KNOW? *The Nile River flooded every year.*

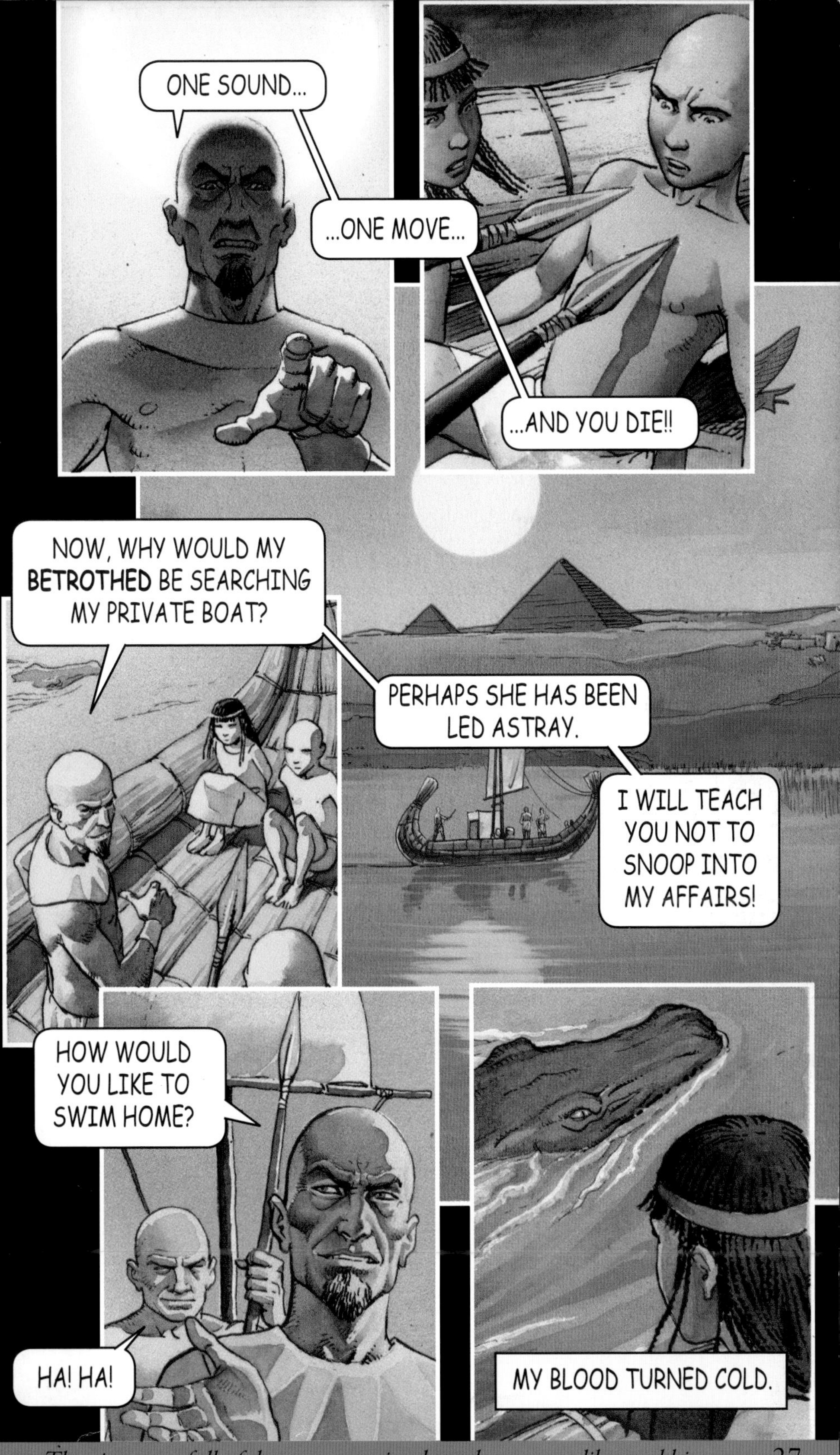
ONE SOUND...
...ONE MOVE...
...AND YOU DIE!!
NOW, WHY WOULD MY **BETROTHED** BE SEARCHING MY PRIVATE BOAT?
PERHAPS SHE HAS BEEN LED ASTRAY.
I WILL TEACH YOU NOT TO SNOOP INTO MY AFFAIRS!
HOW WOULD YOU LIKE TO SWIM HOME?
HA! HA!
MY BLOOD TURNED COLD.

The river was full of dangerous animals such as crocodiles and hippos.

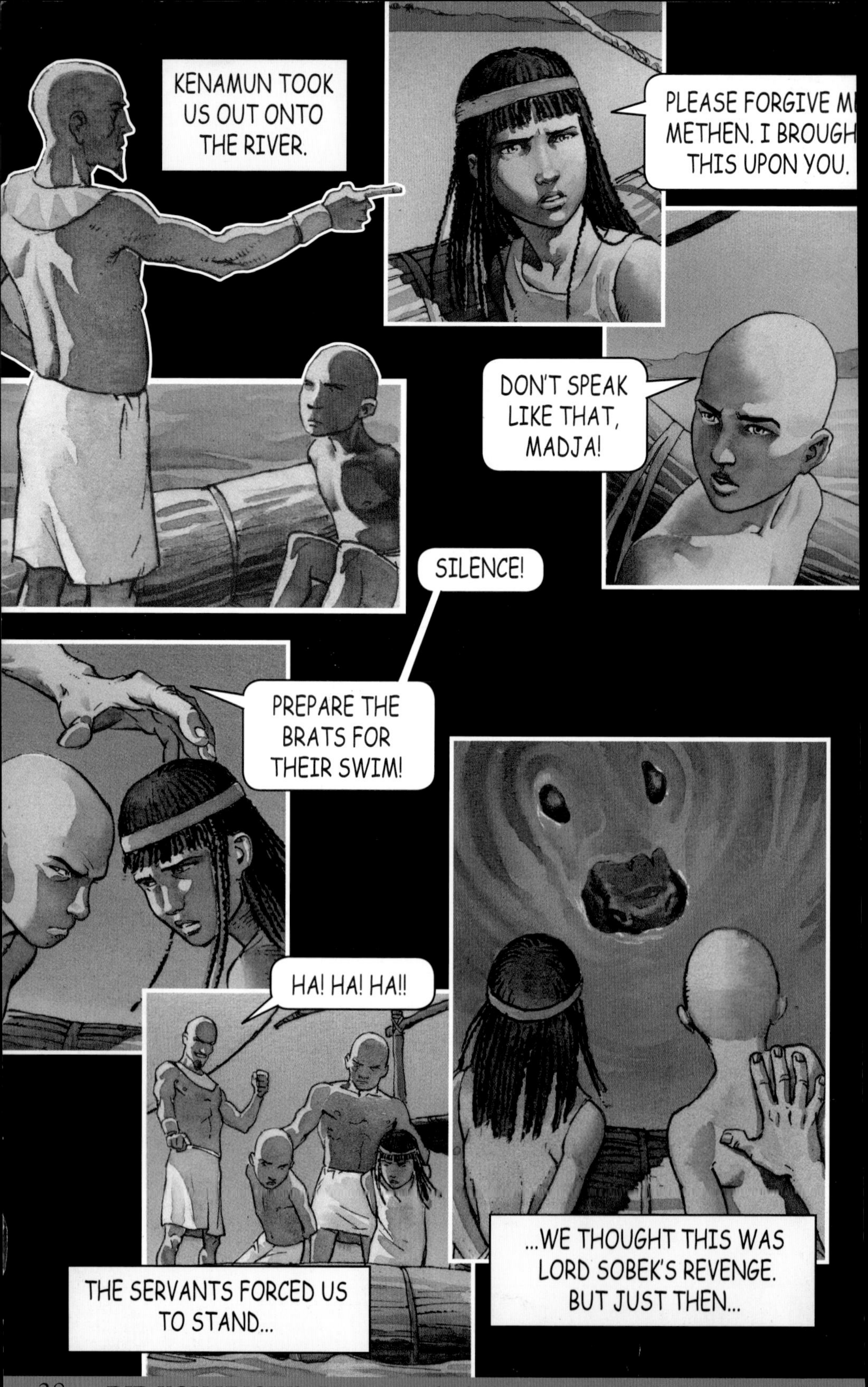
KENAMUN TOOK US OUT ONTO THE RIVER.
PLEASE FORGIVE M METHEN. I BROUGH THIS UPON YOU.
DON'T SPEAK LIKE THAT, MADJA!
SILENCE!
PREPARE THE BRATS FOR THEIR SWIM!
HA! HA! HA!!
THE SERVANTS FORCED US TO STAND...
...WE THOUGHT THIS WAS LORD SOBEK'S REVENGE. BUT JUST THEN...

 DID YOU KNOW? *Hippos weigh about 2,500 pounds (1,000 kg).*

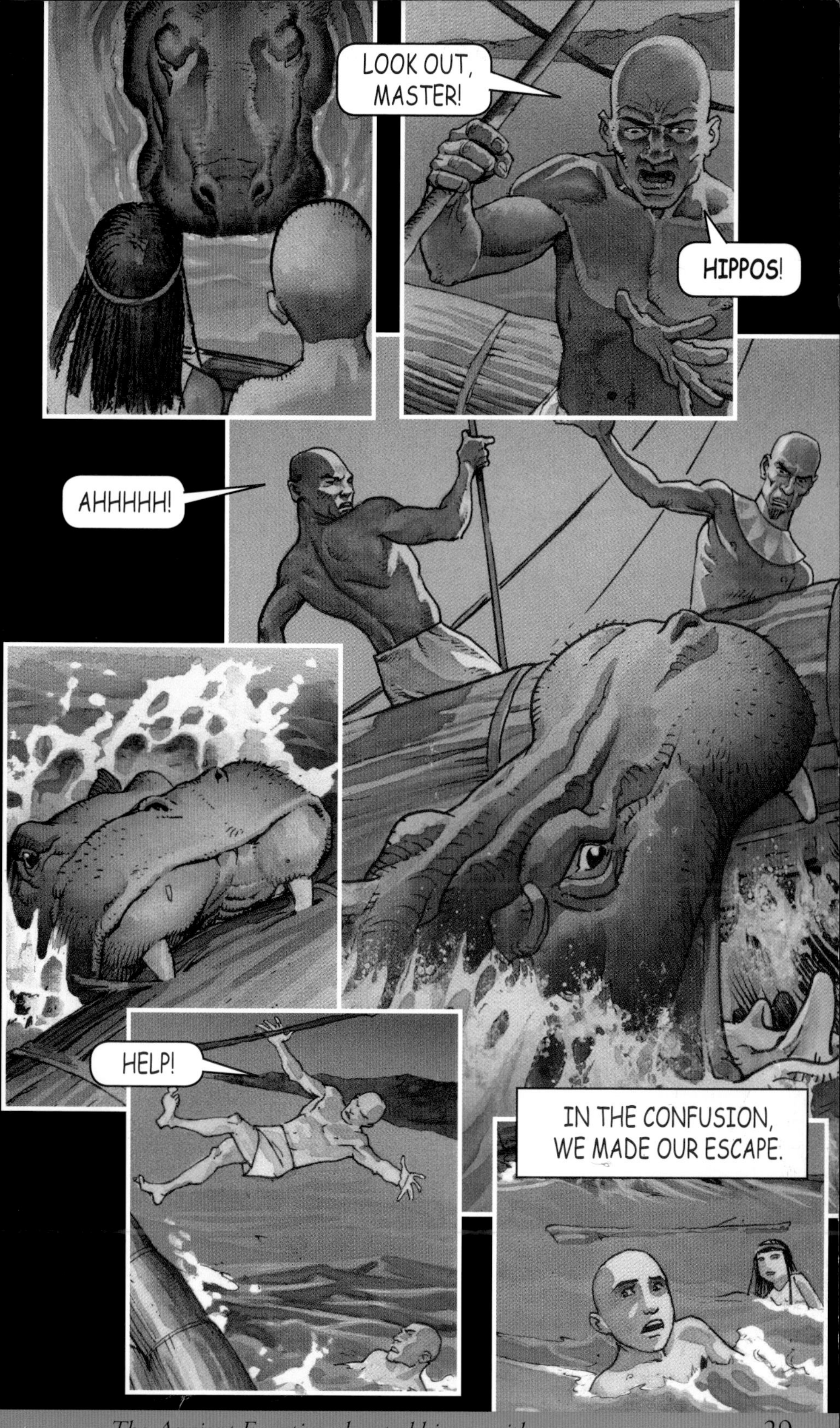
LOOK OUT, MASTER!
HIPPOS!
AHHHHH!
HELP!
IN THE CONFUSION, WE MADE OUR ESCAPE.

The Ancient Egyptians hunted hippos with spears.

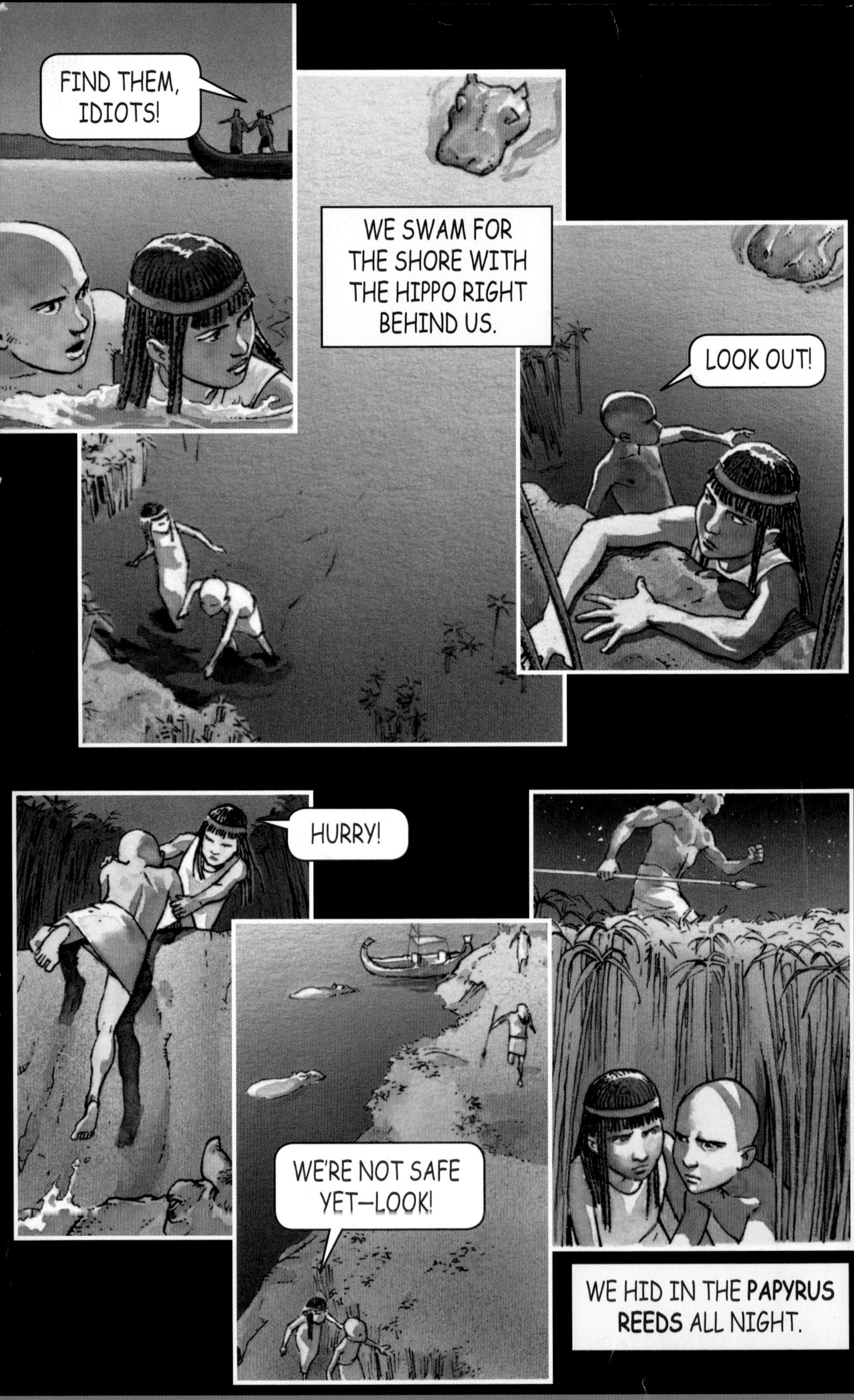
FIND THEM, IDIOTS!
WE SWAM FOR THE SHORE WITH THE HIPPO RIGHT BEHIND US.
LOOK OUT!
HURRY!
WE'RE NOT SAFE YET—LOOK!
WE HID IN THE **PAPYRUS REEDS** ALL NIGHT.

 DID YOU KNOW? *Papyrus grows up to 10 feet (3 meters) tall.*

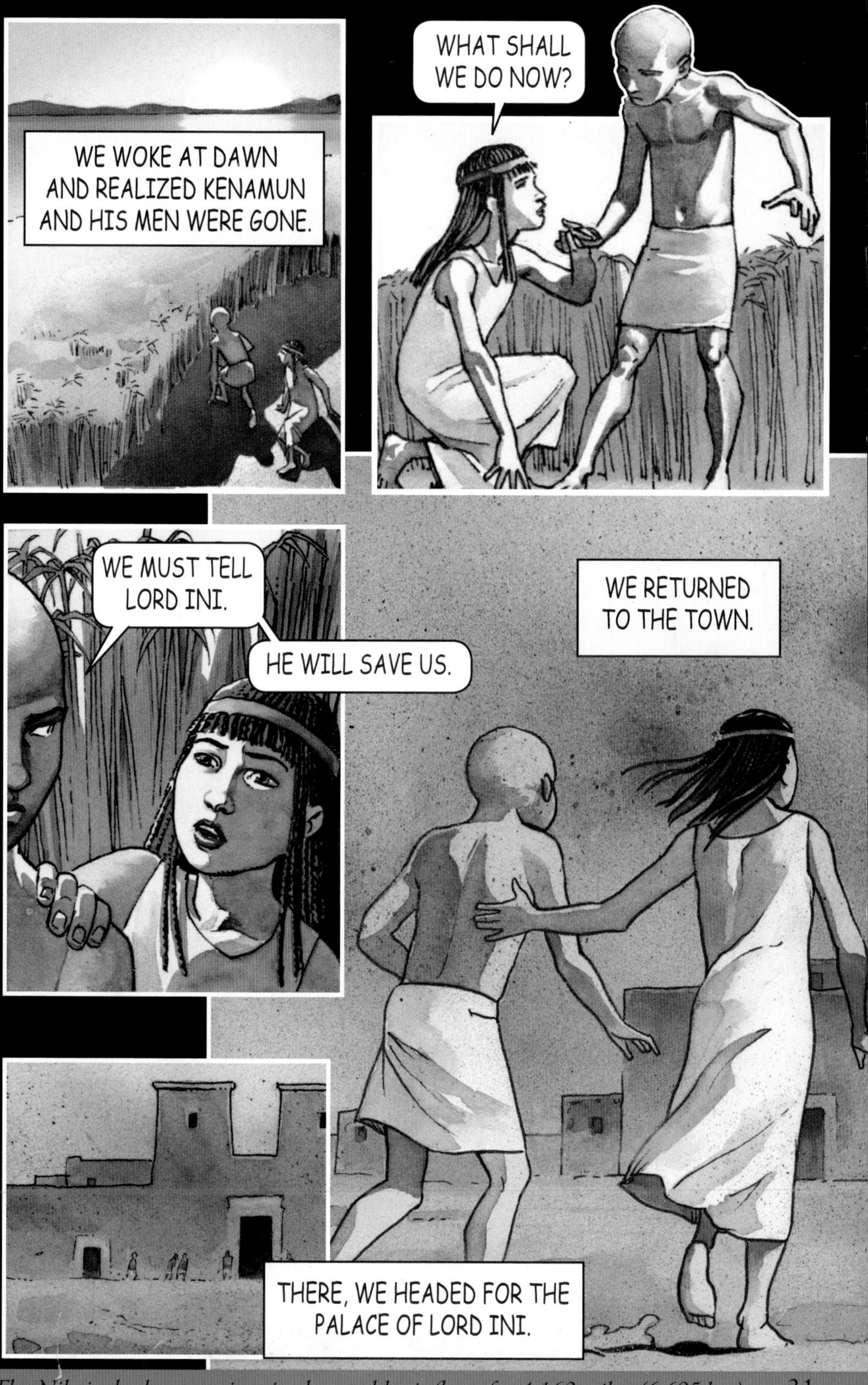
WE WOKE AT DAWN AND REALIZED KENAMUN AND HIS MEN WERE GONE.
WHAT SHALL WE DO NOW?
WE MUST TELL LORD INI.
HE WILL SAVE US.
WE RETURNED TO THE TOWN.
THERE, WE HEADED FOR THE PALACE OF LORD INI.

The Nile is the longest river in the world—it flows for 4,160 miles (6,695 km).

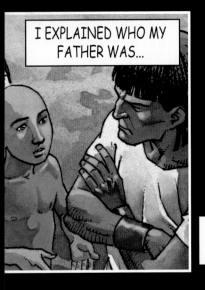

I EXPLAINED WHO MY FATHER WAS...

...AND WE WERE GRANTED AN AUDIENCE WITH HIS LORDSHIP.

WE WERE EXPLAINING OUR INCREDIBLE STORY WHEN...

...TRUMPETS BLARED AND THE DOORS WERE FLUNG OPEN.

IT WAS THE PHARAOH!

THE MIGHTY **SOBEKNEFERU!**

DID YOU KNOW? Sobekneferu was a female pharaoh.

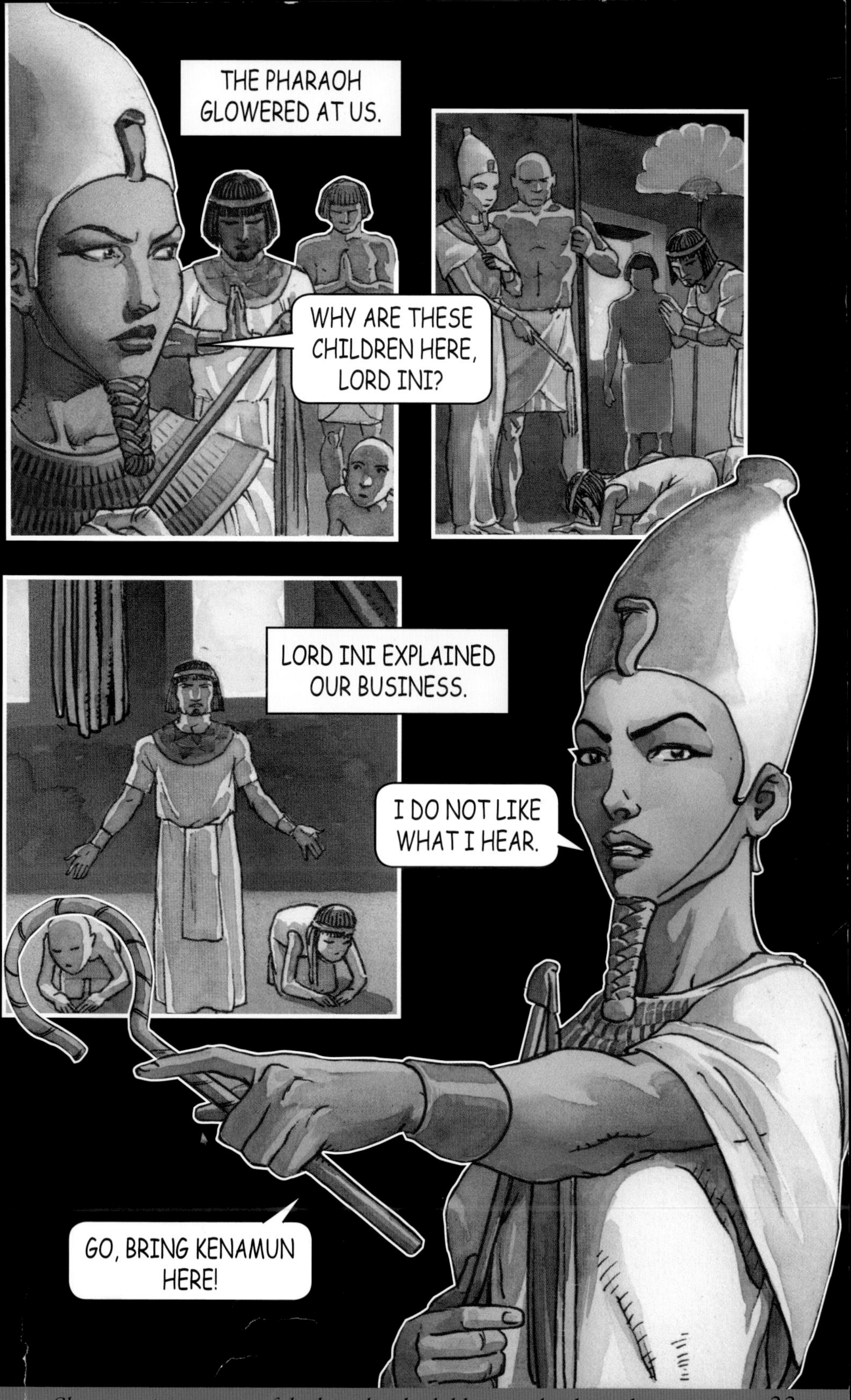
THE PHARAOH GLOWERED AT US.
WHY ARE THESE CHILDREN HERE, LORD INI?
LORD INI EXPLAINED OUR BUSINESS.
I DO NOT LIKE WHAT I HEAR.
GO, BRING KENAMUN HERE!

She sometimes wore a fake beard to look like a male pharaoh.

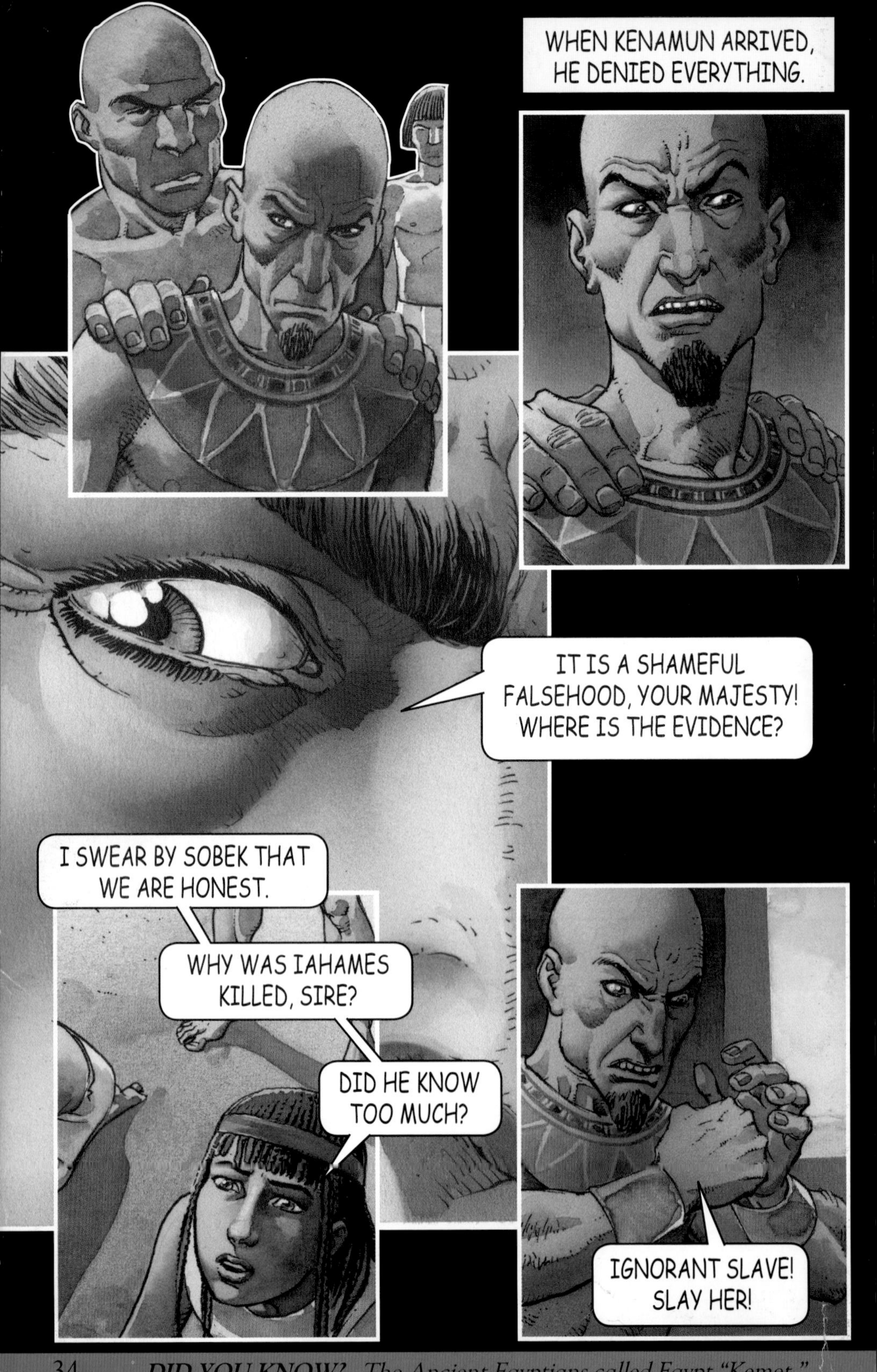
WHEN KENAMUN ARRIVED, HE DENIED EVERYTHING.
IT IS A SHAMEFUL FALSEHOOD, YOUR MAJESTY! WHERE IS THE EVIDENCE?
I SWEAR BY SOBEK THAT WE ARE HONEST.
WHY WAS IAHAMES KILLED, SIRE?
DID HE KNOW TOO MUCH?
IGNORANT SLAVE! SLAY HER!

 DID YOU KNOW? *The Ancient Egyptians called Egypt "Kemet."*

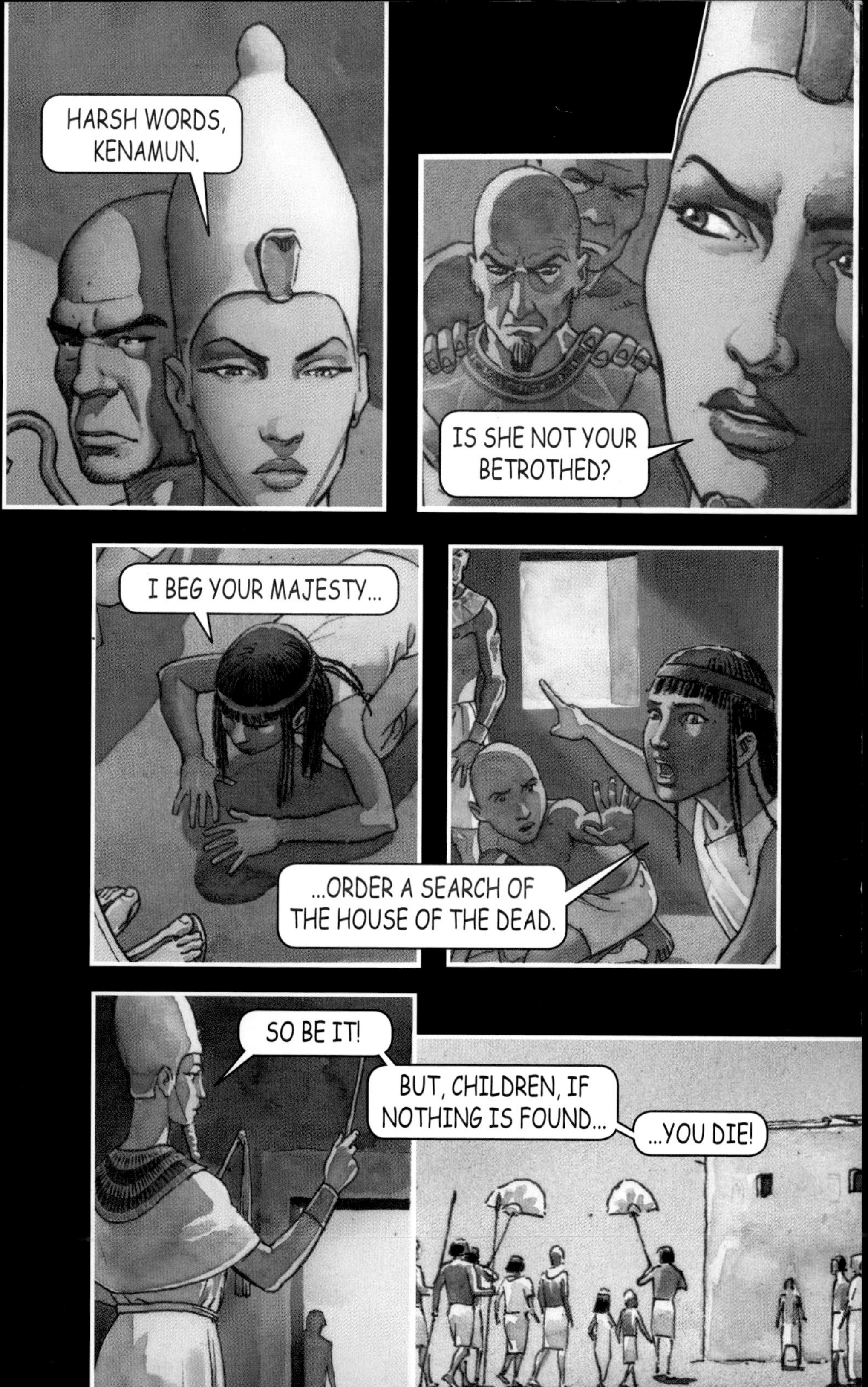
HARSH WORDS, KENAMUN.
IS SHE NOT YOUR BETROTHED?
I BEG YOUR MAJESTY...
...ORDER A SEARCH OF THE HOUSE OF THE DEAD.
SO BE IT!
BUT, CHILDREN, IF NOTHING IS FOUND...
...YOU DIE!

"Kemet" means "black land"—the soil left by the Nile flood water was black.

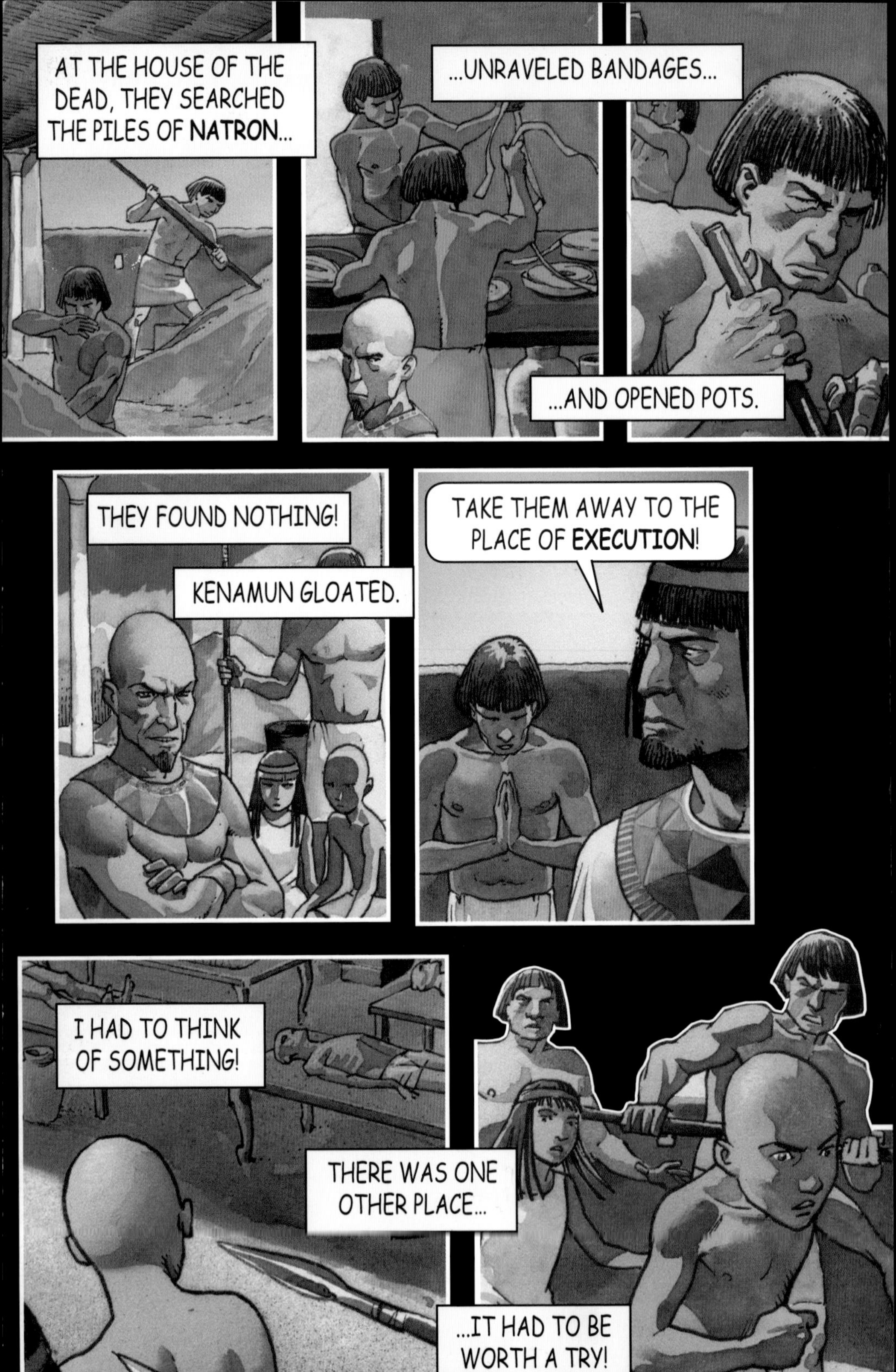
AT THE HOUSE OF THE DEAD, THEY SEARCHED THE PILES OF NATRON...
...UNRAVELED BANDAGES...
...AND OPENED POTS.
THEY FOUND NOTHING!
KENAMUN GLOATED.
TAKE THEM AWAY TO THE PLACE OF EXECUTION!
I HAD TO THINK OF SOMETHING!
THERE WAS ONE OTHER PLACE...
...IT HAD TO BE WORTH A TRY!

DID YOU KNOW? *Natron was used for drying out bodies.*

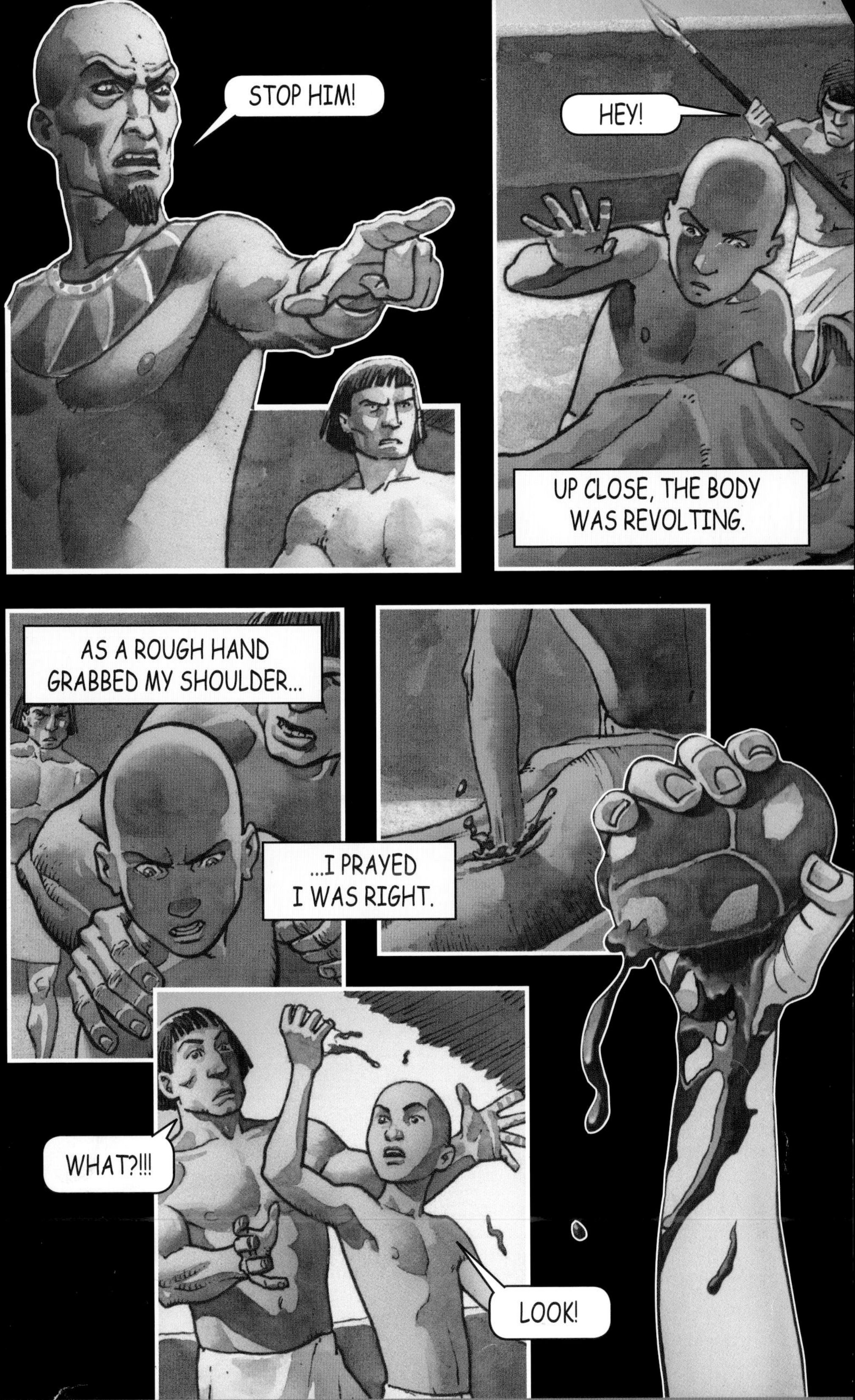
STOP HIM!
HEY!
UP CLOSE, THE BODY WAS REVOLTING.
AS A ROUGH HAND GRABBED MY SHOULDER...
...I PRAYED I WAS RIGHT.
WHAT?!!!
LOOK!

I HANDED THE **PRECIOUS OBJECT** TO LORD INI.

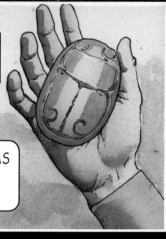

THIS AMULET WAS MADE FOR THE LAST PHARAOH.

I CAN EXPLAIN...

THE SOLDIERS TURNED TO KENAMUN.

SUDDENLY, HE PUSHED LORD INI AWAY...

...KNOCKED OVER A TABLE OF NATRON POTS...

DID YOU KNOW? An amulet was meant to bring good luck.

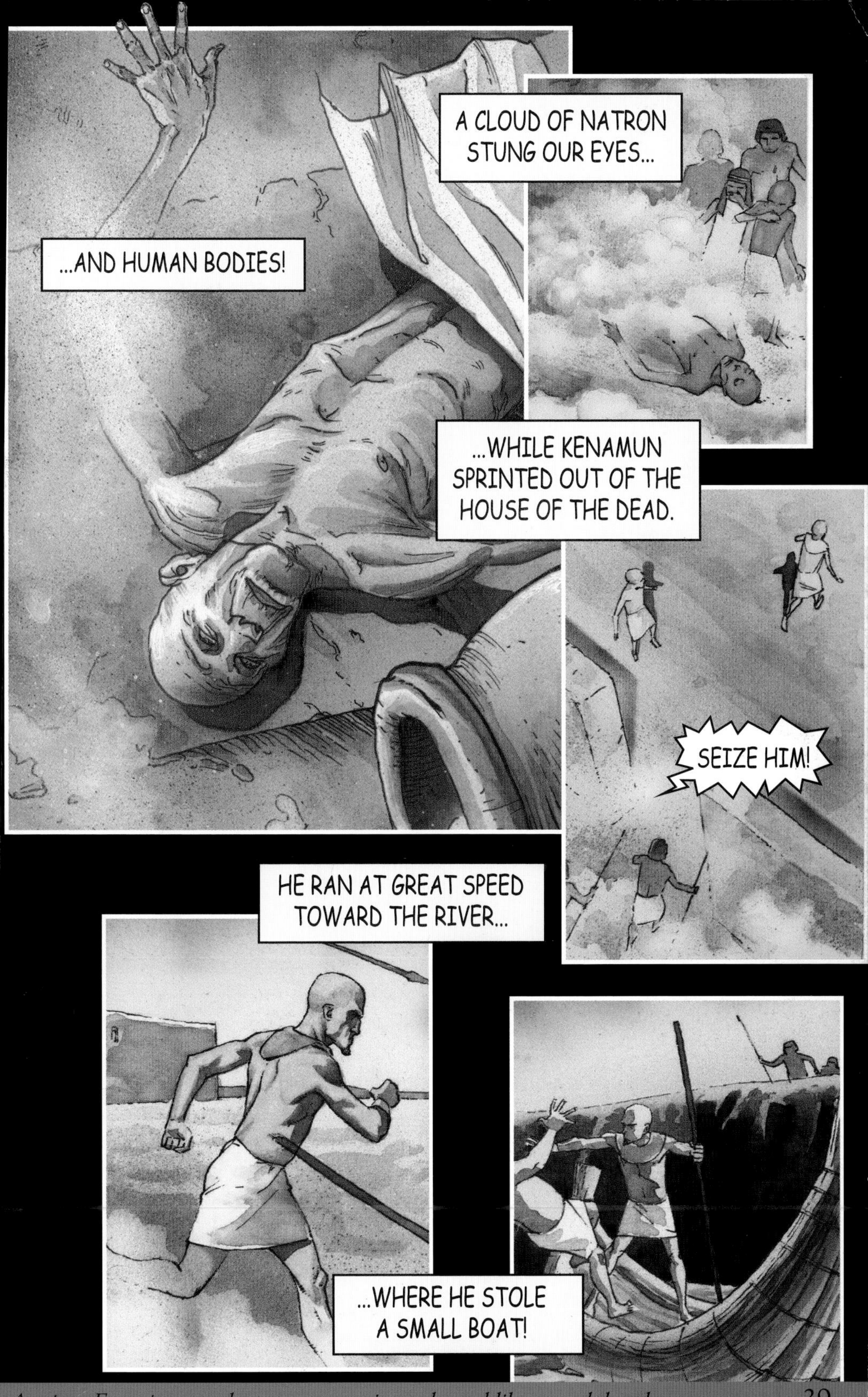
...AND HUMAN BODIES!
A CLOUD OF NATRON STUNG OUR EYES...
...WHILE KENAMUN SPRINTED OUT OF THE HOUSE OF THE DEAD.
SEIZE HIM!
HE RAN AT GREAT SPEED TOWARD THE RIVER...
...WHERE HE STOLE A SMALL BOAT!

Ancient Egyptian amulets were sometimes shaped like scarab beetles.

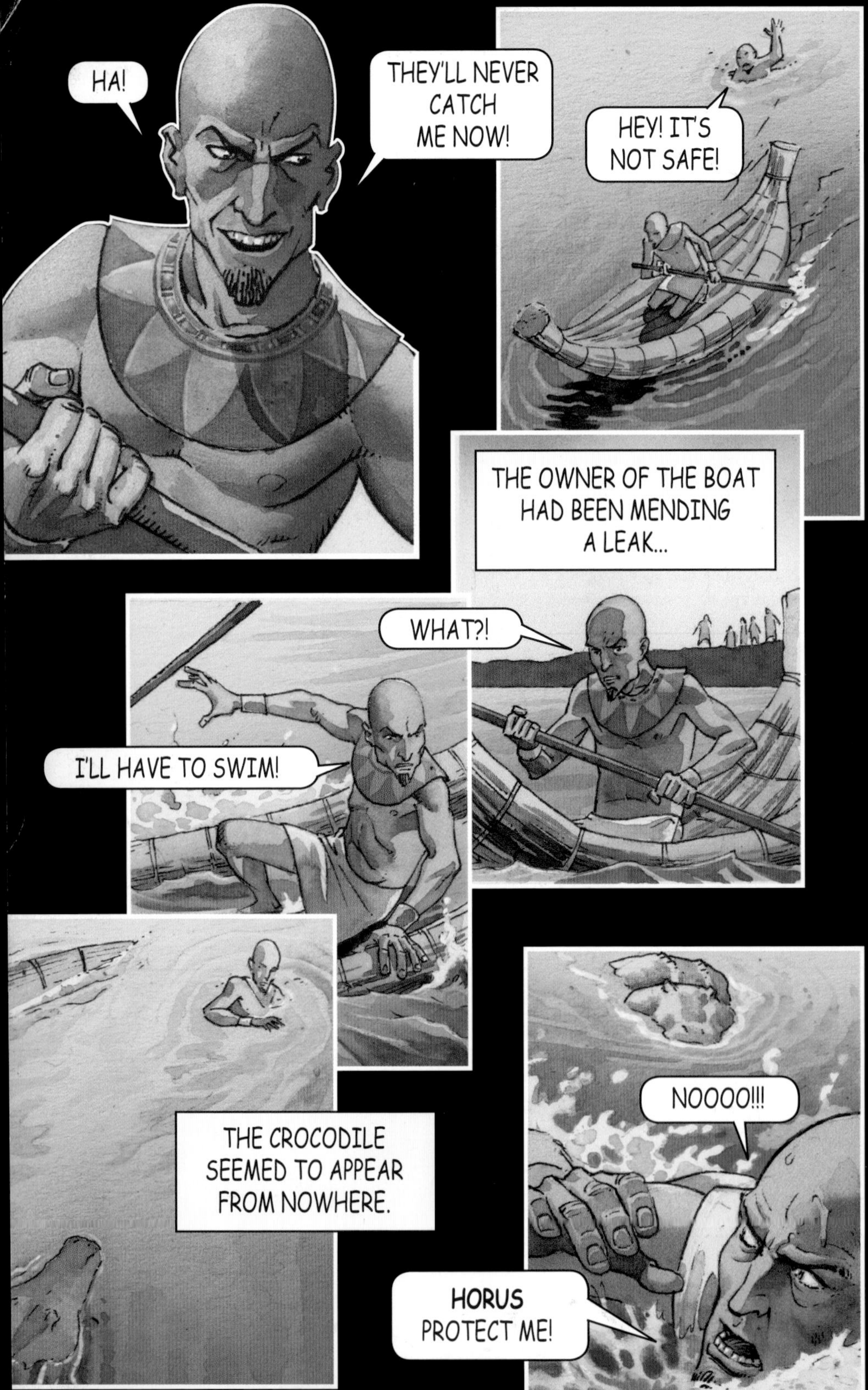
HA!
THEY'LL NEVER CATCH ME NOW!
HEY! IT'S NOT SAFE!
THE OWNER OF THE BOAT HAD BEEN MENDING A LEAK...
WHAT?!
I'LL HAVE TO SWIM!
THE CROCODILE SEEMED TO APPEAR FROM NOWHERE.
NOOOO!!!
HORUS PROTECT ME!

 DID YOU KNOW? *Small reed boats were pushed along with poles.*

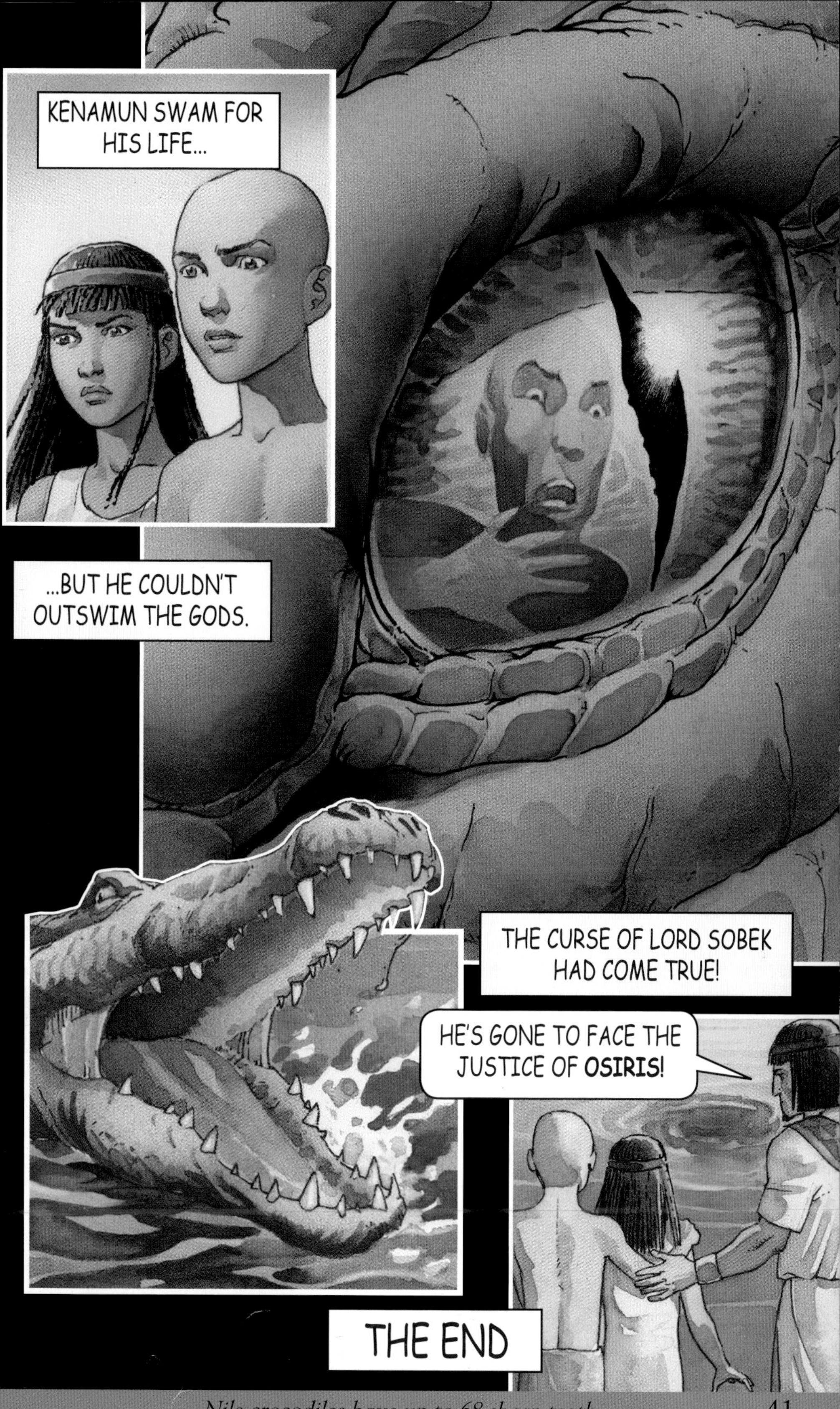
KENAMUN SWAM FOR HIS LIFE...
...BUT HE COULDN'T OUTSWIM THE GODS.
THE CURSE OF LORD SOBEK HAD COME TRUE!
HE'S GONE TO FACE THE JUSTICE OF **OSIRIS**!
THE END

King Menes
unites Egypt
3100

Pharaoh Sobekneferu
comes to the throne
c. 1799

Death of Pharaoh
Rameses III
1153

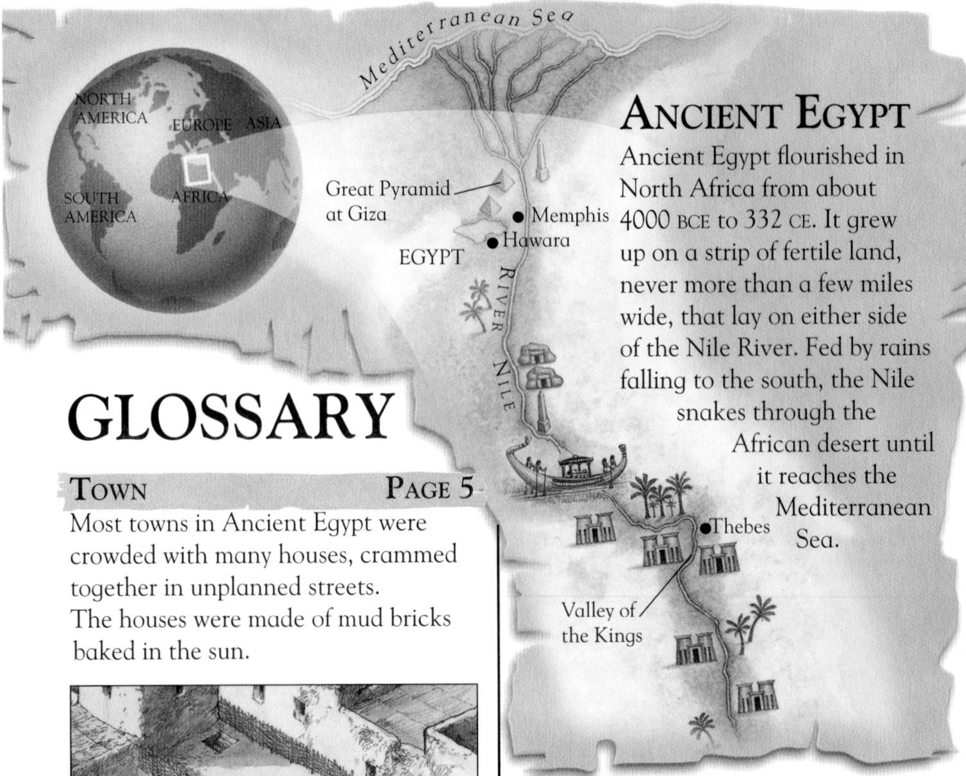

3000 BCE (BEFORE COMMON ERA)   2000 BCE   YOU ARE HERE   1000 BCE

Mediterranean Sea

NORTH AMERICA
EUROPE ASIA
SOUTH AMERICA
AFRICA

Great Pyramid
at Giza

● Memphis
● Hawara

EGYPT

RIVER NILE

●Thebes

Valley of
the Kings

ANCIENT EGYPT

Ancient Egypt flourished in North Africa from about 4000 BCE to 332 CE. It grew up on a strip of fertile land, never more than a few miles wide, that lay on either side of the Nile River. Fed by rains falling to the south, the Nile snakes through the African desert until it reaches the Mediterranean Sea.

GLOSSARY

TOWN   PAGE 5

Most towns in Ancient Egypt were crowded with many houses, crammed together in unplanned streets.
The houses were made of mud bricks baked in the sun.

SOBEK TEMPLE   PAGE 6

Sobek was the crocodile god. He was praised all over Egypt in temples, where priests guarded, cared for, and worshipped the god's image day and night. The priests even prepared meals for the god.

Picture of Sobek on
the temple wall

PHARAOH   PAGE 6

At the top of Egyptian society was the king called a pharaoh. He was considered a god by the Egyptians and above the normal rules of society. Most pharaohs were men, but a few women ruled Ancient Egypt at different times.

Female pharaoh
Hatshepsut

42

Roman Empire collapsing

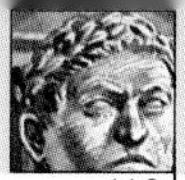

410

Columbus sails to America

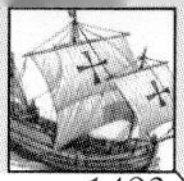

1492

US astronauts land on the Moon

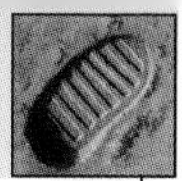

1969

TIMELINE

1 CE (COMMON ERA) 1000 CE 2000 CE

MARRIAGE PAGE 9

Most marriages in Ancient Egypt were arranged by the girl's father and mother. Girls would marry at around 13 years of age and boys at 16. A scribe could draw up a contract giving equal rights to husband and wife.

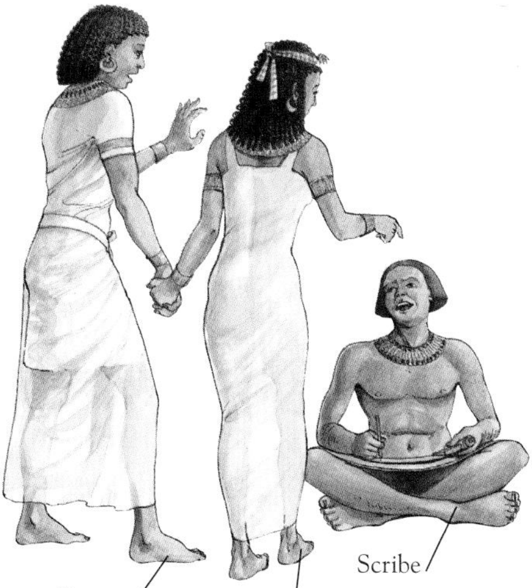

Groom

Bride

Scribe

CHIEF EMBALMER PAGE 7

The Chief Embalmer was in charge of mummifying bodies to preserve them. The Ancient Egyptians believed this helped people live forever. The Chief Embalmer wore a jackal's mask that symbolized Anubis, the god of the dead.

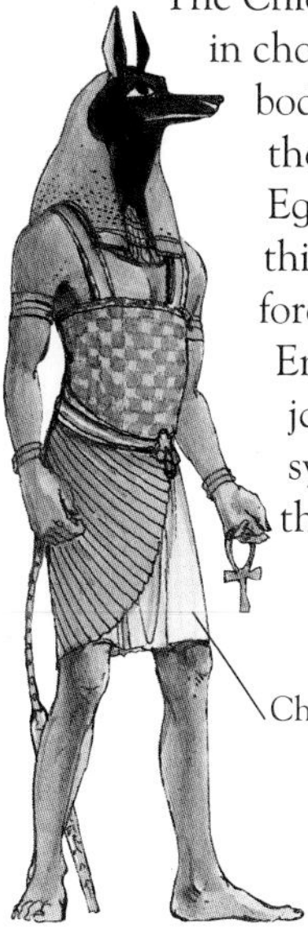

Chief Embalmer

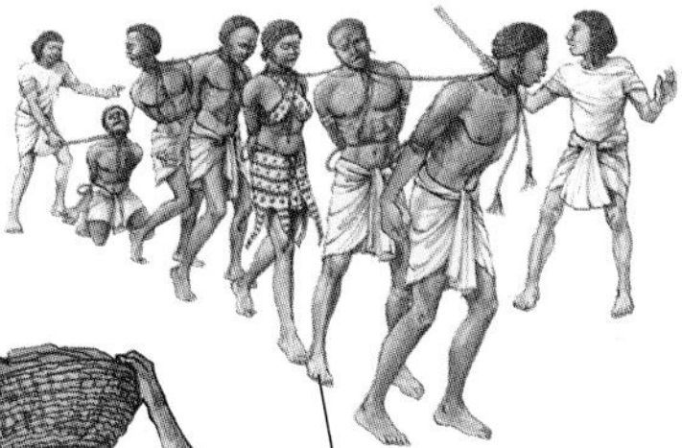

Prisoners of war

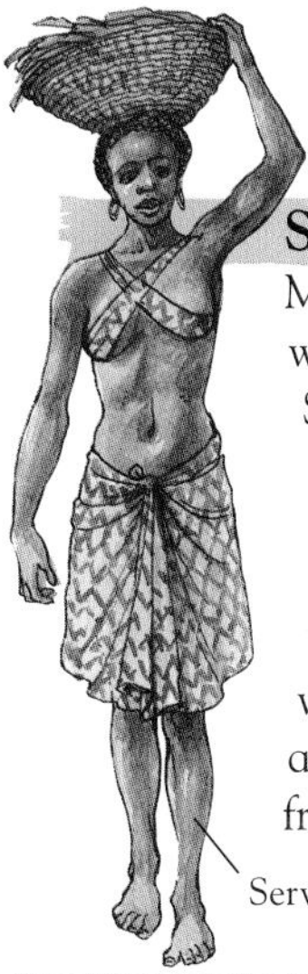

SERVANT PAGE 8

Madja is a servant who works for Lord Ini. Servants were often prisoners brought to Egypt from other countries during wars. They were made to work for rich people and had no rights or freedom.

Servant

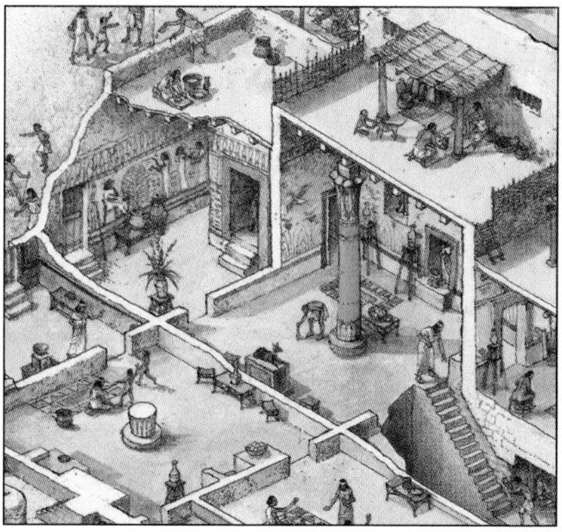

LORD INI'S PALACE PAGE 9

Lord Ini was a rich nobleman who lived in a large palace. The house was expensively decorated, and the interior walls were brightly painted with pictures of people, ducks, and lotus flowers (a type of lily).

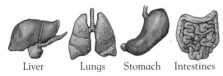

Liver   Lungs   Stomach   Intestines

ENTRAILS   PAGE 9

The entrails are the internal organs of a dead person, such as the intestines. These were removed when a body was mummified and stored in special jars.

The Great Pyramid

The burial chamber

PYRAMID   PAGE 11

The pyramids were burial tombs for the pharaohs and their queens. The biggest one ever built was the Great Pyramid built during the reign of Pharaoh Khufu (2589–2566 BCE).

TOMB ROBBERS   PAGE 13

The pyramids were full of valuable things that the pharaoh might need in the afterlife. Although the tombs had secret passages and rooms, they were easy for robbers to dig their way into.

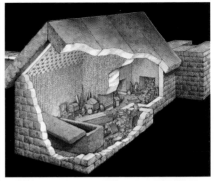

BURIAL CHAMBER   PAGE 15

The body of the pharaoh was buried in the burial chamber hidden deep inside the pyramid. Its whereabouts were meant to be a secret, but since many helped build the temple, the room was often easy for robbers to find.

A scribe writing hieroglyphics

WRITING   PAGE 15

Ancient Egyptian writing was a type of picture writing called hieroglyphics. Only scribes like Methen could read and write.

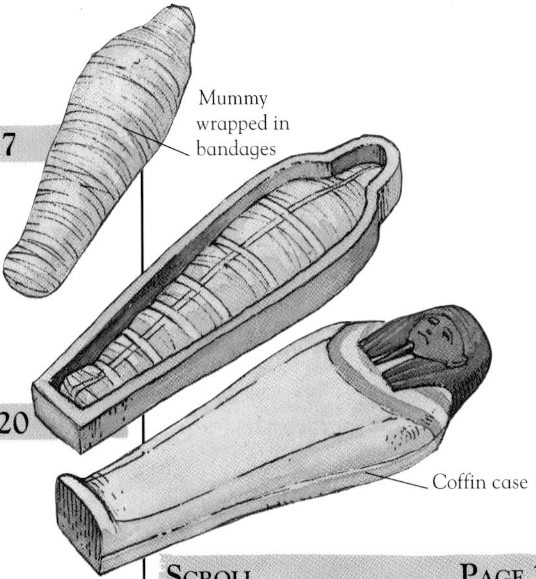
Mummy wrapped in bandages
Coffin case

COFFIN PAGE 17

The mummy was placed in a wooden coffin case that was often shaped like a person. The coffin was often painted with pictures and hieroglyphics.

MUMMIES PAGE 20

The embalmed bodies of the dead were called mummies. After they were dried out and the organs removed, the bodies were usually wrapped in bandages.

SOLDIERS PAGE 20

Soldiers were workers forced to serve the pharaoh. They carried spears and shields but wore little armor.

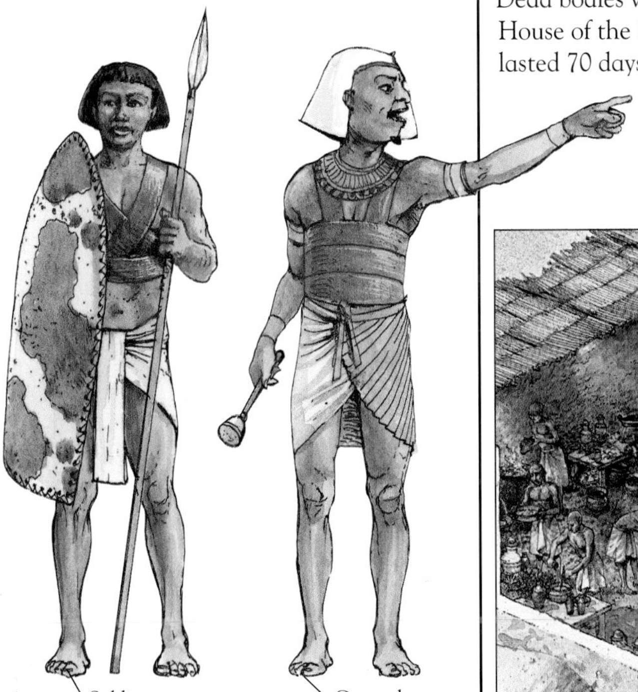

Soldier General

SCROLL PAGE 21

Scribes wrote on sheets of papyrus paper that were rolled up into scrolls. Papyrus was a plant that grew beside the Nile River.

HOUSE OF THE DEAD PAGE 20

Dead bodies were mummified in the House of the Dead in a ritual that lasted 70 days. They were dried so that they did not rot and then usually wrapped in bandages.

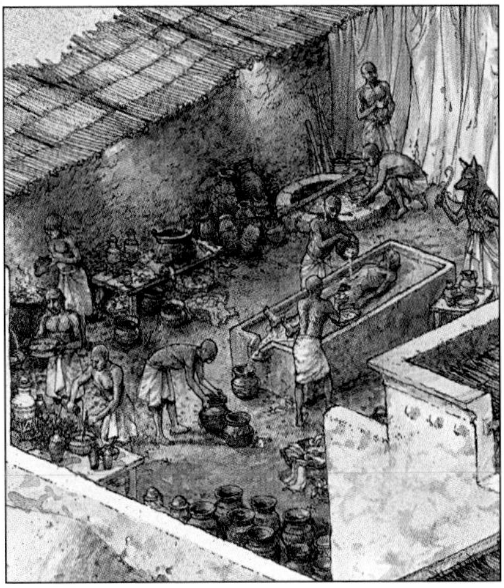

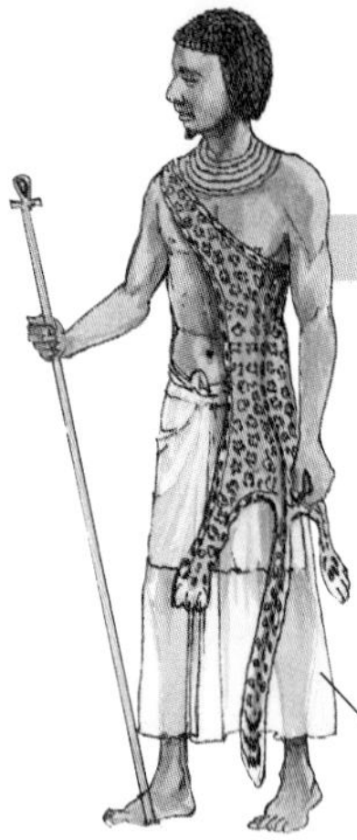
Priest

PRIEST — PAGE 22

Priests like Methen's father performed important religious ceremonies, or rituals. They were important people in Egyptian life.

OFFERINGS — PAGE 22

The priests prepared food and other offerings for the gods. Sobek, the crocodile god, was offered honey cakes and meat.

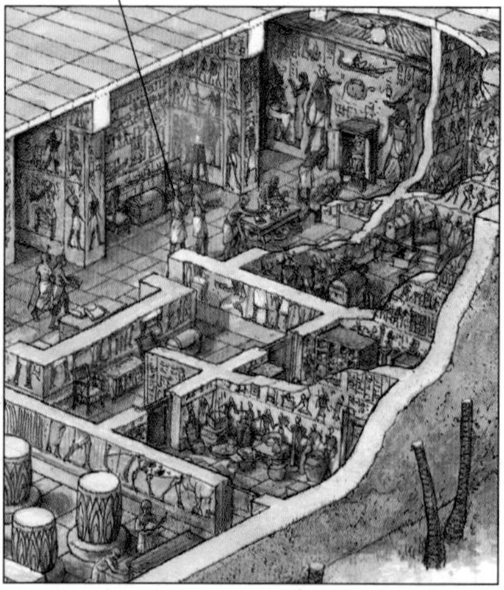
Only the priests could approach the shrine of Sobek

AVENGED — PAGE 23

Methen's father believes the god Sobek will harm the pyramid thieves in return for their wrongdoing, which means Sobek will be avenged.

SACRILEGE — PAGE 23

Offending a god is called sacrilege. Methen and Madja believe they offended the god Sobek by entering the pyramid and breaking a coffin. They believe they were cursed by him.

BOAT — PAGE 24

Nile boats were made of bundles of papyrus reeds. Cargo boats transported heavy goods such as building stone.

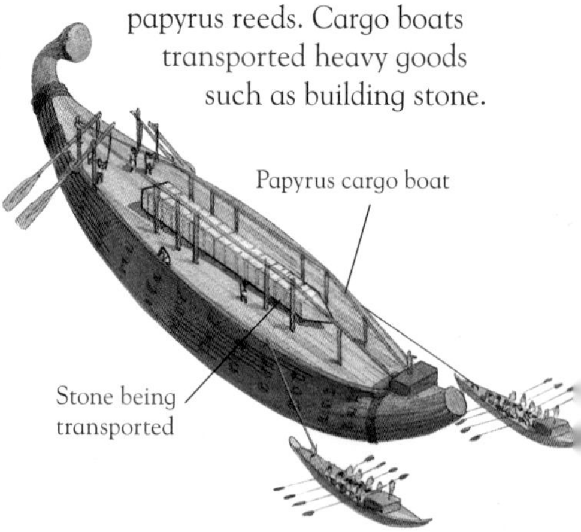
Papyrus cargo boat
Stone being transported

THE NILE — PAGE 24

The civilization of Ancient Egypt depended on the Nile River. Every year, the river flooded the surrounding countryside, making the land better for growing crops when the water receded.

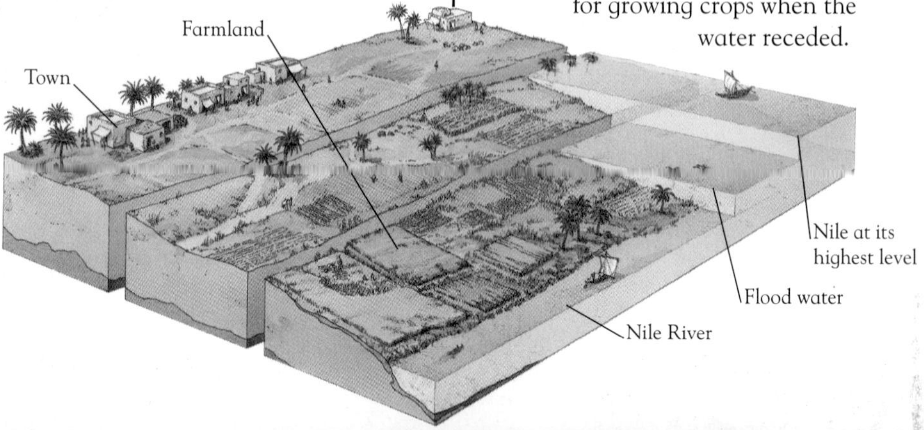
Farmland
Town
Nile at its highest level
Flood water
Nile River

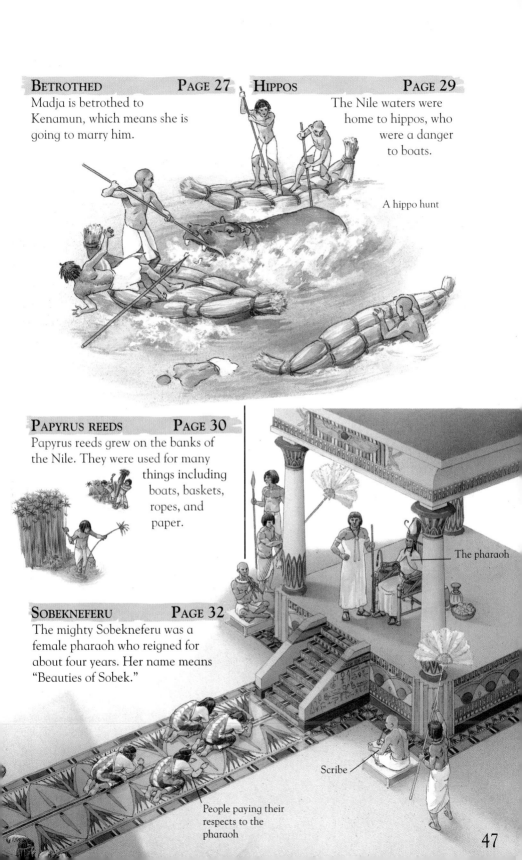

Betrothed Page 27

Madja is betrothed to Kenamun, which means she is going to marry him.

Hippos Page 29

The Nile waters were home to hippos, who were a danger to boats.

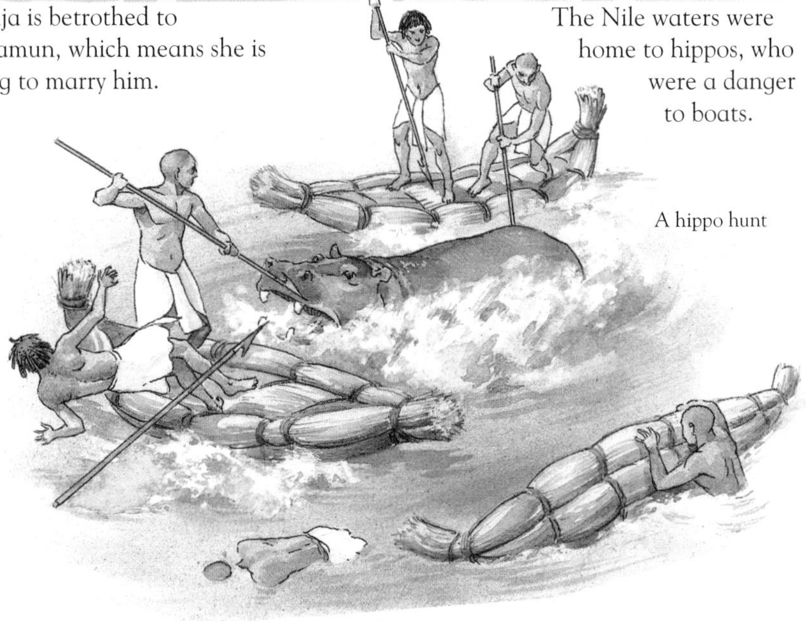

A hippo hunt

Papyrus reeds Page 30

Papyrus reeds grew on the banks of the Nile. They were used for many things including boats, baskets, ropes, and paper.

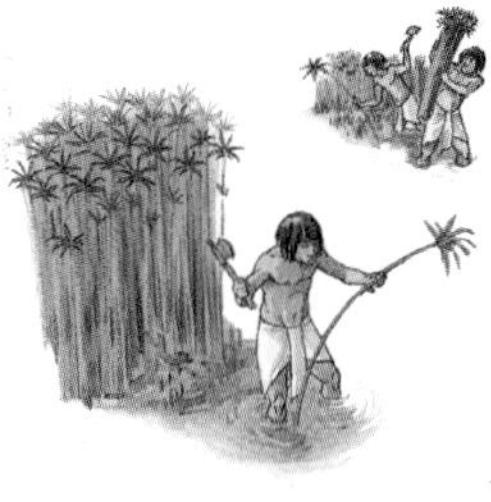

Sobekneferu Page 32

The mighty Sobekneferu was a female pharaoh who reigned for about four years. Her name means "Beauties of Sobek."

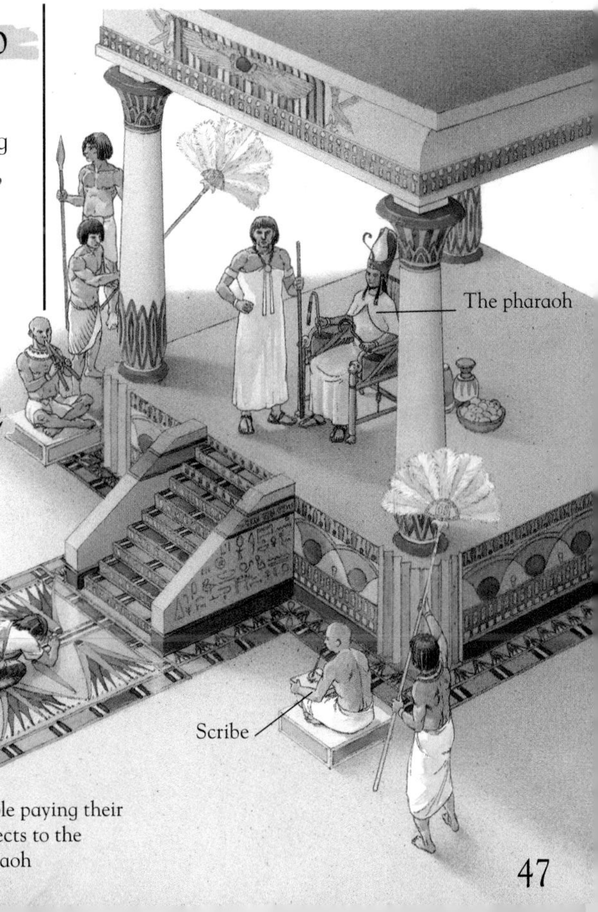

The pharaoh

Scribe

People paying their respects to the pharaoh

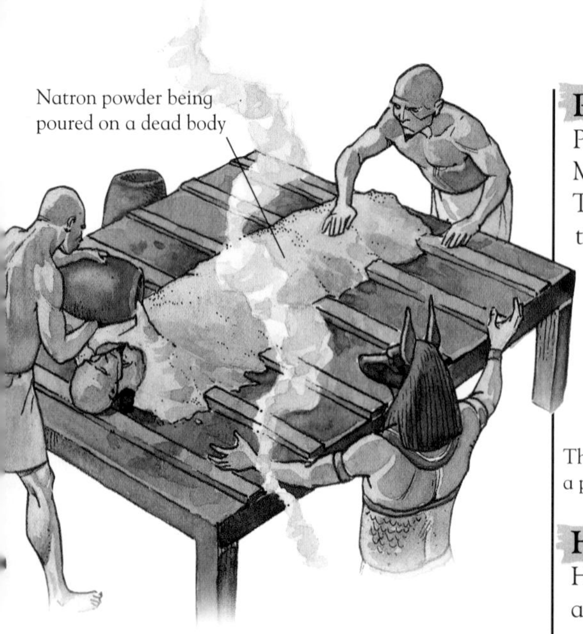
Natron powder being
poured on a dead body

Natron — Page 36

Natron was a saltlike substance used to dry out dead bodies when they were being made into mummies. The white powder was mined from dry lake beds near the Nile River.

Execution — Page 36

The most common punishment in Egypt was beating, but serious crimes could be punished by execution, which means being put to death.

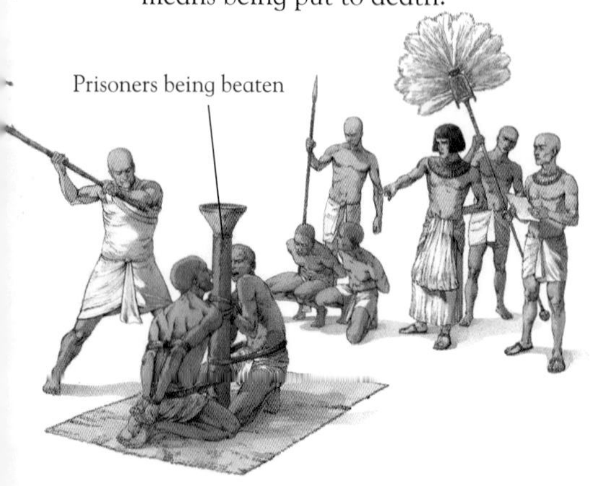
Prisoners being beaten

Precious object — Page 38

Precious objects, such as the amulet Methen found, were valuable items. They were put in the tomb in case the pharaoh needed them in the afterlife.

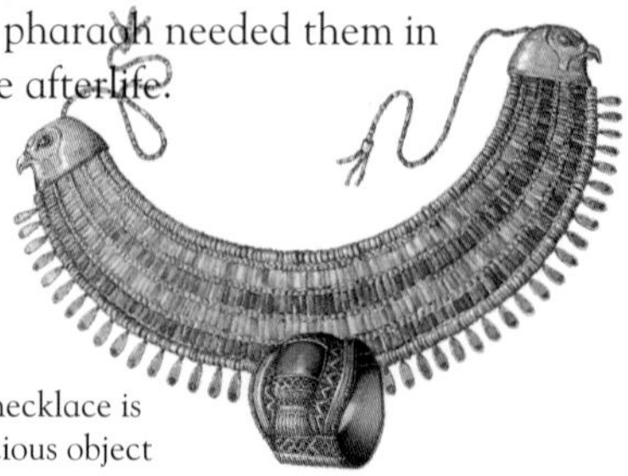

This necklace is a precious object

Horus — Page 40

Horus was an Egyptian god with a hawk's head. The Horus-eye was a symbol of healing and protection.

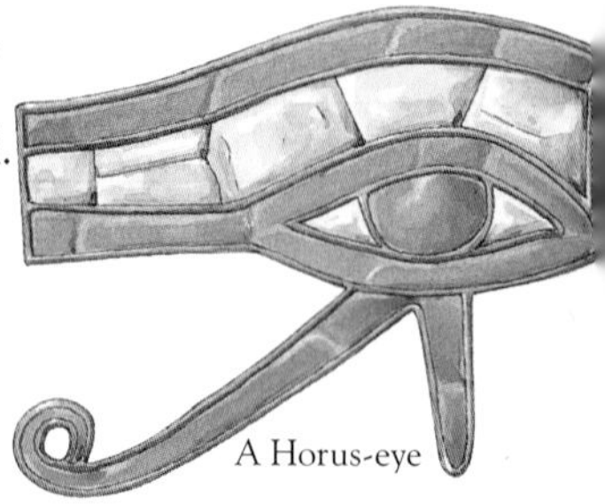

A Horus-eye

Osiris — Page 41

Osiris was the god of death and rebirth. He judged the dead in the Underworld. Only those who had led good lives were granted eternal life.

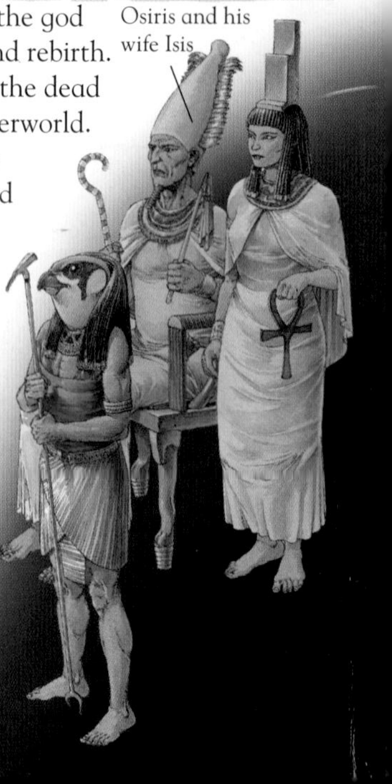
Osiris and his
wife Isis
Horus